Cataloged for Catastrophe

AMY E. LILLY

DEDICATION

For Lily and Natalie aka The Diva Girls

ACKNOWLEDGMENTS

A big thank you to Shari Flynn for her amazing work on my cover and my husband for always supporting my writing journey.

Chapter One

"I think it's a mistake to dig up your yard, Phee. It might mess up the positive Mother Nature vibes. Disturb the bees," Juliet said, sipping her cup of herbal tea.

"Nonsense," I replied. "It's not every day my baby sister gets married. By the time I'm done with this place, it will be the ideal spot for your wedding."

Despite Juliet's protests, I knew she was happy I had agreed to host her wedding in my backyard. Her original plan to hold the wedding at the lake had been thrown out the window when an ugly red algae bloom had taken over. The stink emanating from the water could bring a grown man to his knees.

The two men I hired to tear down the old garden shed in the backyard loaded the last scraps of wood into the back of their beat-up Chevy pickup. The elder Mr. Gant stuck plugs into his ears and started the jackhammer.

"If the neighbors aren't already awake, they will be with that thing running," I said, putting my fingers into my ears to block the noise.

"You want to go running? When have you ever wanted to run?"

I raised my voice so she could hear me over the racket. "I said... oh, never mind."

The jackhammer made quick work of the cement pad. The younger Mr. Gant wheeled load after load of cement rubble to the construction dumpster. When he bent over to pick up a large chunk of cement, he stopped and leaned down to peer at the ground.

"What's he doing?" Juliet squinted. She needed glasses, but despite her protestations, I knew her vanity kept her from getting a pair. She walked off the porch and across the yard to get a closer look.

I followed her down the steps to see what was going on.

"Phee, I don't think you should come over here," the elder Mr. Gant said. His wrinkled, sunburned face had a grayish cast.

"Why? What's wrong?" I asked. I tried to move closer, but he held up his hand to stop me.

"It's a skull, Phee. We found a human skull."

Two hours later, my backyard was no longer a wedding venue in progress. Instead, it was an active crime scene. Well, I assume it was an active crime scene since my boyfriend, who was also a sheriff's deputy, was currently speaking to a crime scene technician who had arrived from nearby Burlington to process the yard.

"This is a sign from the goddess," Juliet wailed. She took a big sip of her wine. Shortly after the skull had been found, her cup of herbal tea had been dumped down the sink and a bottle of cabernet opened. "I knew getting married was something other people did. I should just live in sin until the day I die."

"Maybe it's an old grave from when the pioneers traveled through here on their way to Oregon," I said. I took the glass of wine from her hand and drained it. "I can't believe I have a dead body in my backyard. Fritz or Watson could have dug it up and been gnawing on a finger bone in my kitchen."

"Ugh." Juliet wrinkled her nose. "I can't… maybe, I can… no, I just can't even think about how we'll be able to cleanse this place and remove the bad vibes before the wedding. There isn't enough sage in the world to drive this kind of bad juju away."

"You could get married at the church. I'm sure Mom and Dad would be thrilled." I watched them transfer the skeletal remains from the hole in my backyard into a black body bag.

Clint shook the tech's hand and walked over to Juliet and me. "Your yard's a crime scene, Phee. All wedding gazebo plans are delayed for now."

"It isn't an old pioneer grave?" I still held onto a remnant of hope that I could keep the wedding on track and get Juliet and Wade to the altar without any more problems. My sister was as skittish about traditions as a raccoon in a forest full of coonhounds.

"I don't think pioneers wore bell-bottomed jeans, big silver and turquoise belt buckles, and carried lighters in their pants pocket. This body is newer than that."

"Home burial?" I asked as the hope slipped through my fingers.

"A bullet in the skull pretty much ruled that out." Clint held up an evidence bag with a slug. "It's murder, Phee."

Chapter Two

"No."

"But–" I tried to protest.

"I said no." Juliet crossed her arms. "I'm not getting married in the church. It is so establishment, and you know that's not me. The reverend said he would go to whatever location I choose. First, the lake turns blood red with algae, and now a dead body turns up in your yard. It will probably rain frogs next. It's a portent."

"Juliet's right," Willow shook her head full of dreadlocks. She had dyed them a shocking shade of teal. "Until we remove whatever curse hovers over the nuptials, she and Wade shouldn't decide on a new location."

I sighed. I often wondered how someone as down-to-earth and practical as me got a sister like Juliet. Not a superstitious person by nature, I had to admit that things were not looking good for holding a wedding within the next two months. "Fine. How do we remove the curse?" I took a sip of the tea Willow had given me and almost spat it out. I did a hard swallow. "What is this?"

"A special mixture of herbs designed to remove hexes. As a bonus, it's good for the skin." Willow took a sip and smacked her lips. "I've got some friends working on the algae bloom, but the spirits say we need to find out what happened to the man buried in your backyard. It's his spirit causing discord in your aura, Phee."

"My aura?"

"You're closely tied to this wedding. Juliet is your sister. Wade works for you. The wedding venue is your house." She ticked her point off one by one on her fingers. "It makes sense it's you who disrupted the spirits."

"I have to have Phee in the wedding. She's my sister. No Phee means no wedding. Period." Juliet's blue eyes filled with tears.

I reached over and hugged her. "No worries. We'll solve the murder, and the wedding will be back on."

Juliet sniffled. "We don't even know who the dead guy is. Where would we even start?"

"I'm sure the sheriff's office will identify the remains. I'll talk to Clint this evening and find out what they've discovered. They might even have this murder solved by dinner."

***

My earlier confidence faded over the tuna noodle casserole that evening. The fishy dish was one of Clint's favorite comfort foods. He loved my secret ingredient that wasn't so secret, crushed potato chips on top. To sweeten the interrogation, I baked turtle brownies for dessert.

"This is an active investigation," Clint said. He scooped up the last forkful of casserole, then looked around the kitchen in search of a second helping.

I stood up and put a spoonful of casserole on his plate. "Juliet won't get married until we solve the murder. Willow has her convinced I have a curse hanging over my head that is transferring itself to her wedding. I'm only curious if you've discovered anything about the dead body yet."

"You," Clint pointed his fork in my direction, "have to stay out of this. After the shenanigans in Arizona, you promised to stay away from all things related to death, murder, or felony crimes."

"True, but that was because I didn't want to risk getting injured, maimed, or murdered. This is clearly a cold case, so I could help by doing research. The library has all the newspapers on microfilm. I could see if anyone went missing around the time of our dead guy. Bell-bottomed jeans were only in fashion for a decade, and I'm the queen of the microfilm."

"While I appreciate your argument, my beautiful but nosy love, I'm still not telling you anything. The sheriff would have my hide. Besides, it's not my case."

"Who's working on it?"

"Lu. The sheriff pulled her off patrol and assigned her this case. She's happy about the change since she had to pull over and find a bathroom every twenty minutes."

Lu was eight months pregnant. We all thought she would go on desk duty sooner, but she insisted she could still ride patrol around the county until the day she gave birth. While I admired her moxie, I knew she hadn't really understood the changes pregnancy would wreak on her body when she said she would give birth on patrol and go right back to work.

I cut a large brownie and put it on a small plate for Clint. "Well, I hope she finds something out soon because, if not, my sister may cancel the wedding altogether."

"You'll leave it alone?" Clint arched his eyebrow.

"I'm sure Lu will have it solved within the week and the wedding will be back on." I gave him my sweetest smile. "Whipped cream?"

The next morning, I gave Clint a kiss and told him to be safe.

"Dinner at Odd Couples tonight?" Clint asked.

"Late dinner? I've got book club this evening and we won't be done until seven o'clock," I said.

"I'll meet you there. Okay if I ask Lu to come? She's been looking a little down. Has she said anything to you?"

"No. I'll stop by on my lunch break and check on her. If something is bothering Lu, she might be more willing to talk without her partner listening in." I fastened silver hoops into my earlobes, then pulled my red curls up into a messy bun.

"No snooping into the skeleton."

"No snooping. Scout's honor," I said, crossing my fingers behind my back. He didn't need to know that I had never made it past my early days as a Brownie. Too much nature and not enough reading. Juliet, however, had stuck with it until she reached middle school.

Chapter Three

I strolled by the sheriff's office on my lunch break when I spotted Lu getting out of her car. Actually, she tried to get out of her car, however, because of her current situation, she was stuck behind the wheel. She attempted to hoist herself out and failed miserably. It reminded me of a turtle I found when I was little. It had somehow tipped over on its back. Even though touching reptiles and amphibians rated high on my list of gross things, I saved him. He repaid my good deed by peeing on my hand.

"Do you need me to help you?" I offered her my hand.

Lu scowled at me. But she was smart enough not to turn down a savior in the form of a short librarian. I tugged, and she popped out of her cruiser like a cork from a good bottle of wine. She quickly smoothed her deputy's uniform and glanced around to make sure no one had been watching. "Thanks. One month, three days, and five hours until this baby is out, and I can be a normal human being," Lu grumbled.

"You have it down to the hour? Babies don't operate that way. He or she will come out when they're ready. It's not a turkey. You can't set a timer and when it dings, the baby comes out," I said. An image of Lu as a turkey with a red pop-up timer on her belly made me snort. I stifled it when I heard a growl from Lu. She had always been prickly, but with the pregnancy hormones in high gear, she was a mama grizzly bear. It didn't help that she sent Anthony away

8

without telling him about their baby. A few times, I had been tempted to call him, but Clint told me to stay out of it. Anthony went back on the campaign trail with the senator after Lu dumped him, and I did not know if he would return to Miller's Cove.

"I counted backwards from the date and time that Anthony and I–well, you know–and based upon my calculations, I will be full term in one month, three days, and five hours." She looked at her watch. "Make that four hours and fifty-five minutes."

When I saw she was serious, I changed the subject. "Juliet wants to call the wedding off."

"Why?" Lu grabbed her lunch box from the front seat of her cruiser and shut the door. "Did she and Wade have a fight?"

"Not at all. Correction. They did when Juliet said she might call off the wedding. She thinks the dead body in my backyard is a sign that the wedding is cursed. She's decided to live in sin rather than risk the wrath of the goddess or whatever deity she's into this month."

Lu sighed. "I can't tell you anything about the investigation, Phee. You know that. The sheriff already read Clint and me the riot act about disclosing information to the public. He wants this case closed in a hurry before tourist season is in full swing."

I put my hand to my chest in mock dismay. "I am shocked that you think I would try to get any information about the case. I just happened to be walking by on my lunch break when I spotted you."

Lu narrowed her eyes at me. "Clint already

9

called me this morning and said you were fishing for information. I've been warned." She pointed her finger at me. "You've been warned,"

Clint outmaneuvered me. If I was going to get this wedding back on track, I needed this murder solved. It's not that I didn't have faith in Clint's and Lu's detecting abilities. I just had greater motivation to solve it in a hurry. "Come on, Lu. It's not like it's a fresh murder or anything. How dangerous could it be? When was this guy killed? The sixties?"

"More like the late seventies," Lu said.

"Aha! So, they have narrowed it down."

"Dang it, Phee. I wasn't even supposed to say that." She put her hand up. "Stop. I'm going inside. My lunch break is over, and I need to get back to digging through missing person files from that time."

"At least tell me how you narrowed it down. Consider it an educational opportunity." I grinned at her. "You know how much I like to learn new things."

"Fine. I don't see how it will hurt." She rubbed her round belly, and I caught a brief glimpse of a smile before it disappeared. "I stayed up to all hours of the night researching fashion. The style and brand of bell-bottomed jeans wasn't manufactured until 1978. Plus, we went through the money we found in the pockets and scattered in the grave. There were no coins after 1979. I pulled the building permit records and the shed wasn't built until 1990."

"So that gives you a fairly clear window of when this guy went into the ground. Between 1979 and 1990. Interesting."

"I've really got to go, Phee. Are we still on for lunch next Saturday?" Lu asked.

"Yes. One o'clock. I'll pick you up."

I gave her a quick wave and hurried back to the library. My own lunch break was over, and I needed to get ready for afternoon story hour. Even though Lu hadn't given me as much information as I wanted, I had everything I needed to start solving this crime. Now, to make a date with a microfilm machine.

Two hours later, the children were gone, the crafts cleaned up, and the library was empty except for Mr. Cobb, who snored in the chair with the day's newspaper still in his hand. A widower, he came every afternoon to read the paper and visit with other local retirees. He would fall asleep and then wake up when our next wave of patrons came in after work.

I went to the filing cabinet in the corner of the genealogy area. The local newspaper digitized the more recent years of the newspaper, but anything prior to the nineties only existed on microfilm. I had applied for a grant from the state to digitize the earlier years, but there was no word if the library won the award. Bigger city libraries and county systems tended to garner the grants sooner than small independent ones like mine.

I loaded a roll from the early half of 1979 onto the reel and fed it through the machine. I skimmed past news regarding the Shah of Iran and President Jimmy Carter's metric initiative. Nothing caught my eye.

I loaded another roll of microfilm. Halfway through, I spotted something. I rewound slowly and stopped. Halfway down the third page, I spotted a photograph of a local band that performed that year at the annual Founder's Day Festival. What caught my eye was a member of the band. He wore a pair of bell-bottomed jeans with a fancy belt buckle. It was hard to tell in the grainy black-and-white photograph, but it looked like a silver and turquoise belt. The caption identified the band as The Screaming Goats, but no names of the band members appeared.

I printed out the page, then continued to skim through the rest of 1979. I chuckled a few times at photographs of big-haired women, and I thanked my lucky stars that makeup trends back then faded. I didn't find any articles about a missing person, male or female, so I decided to call it quits. It was time to wake Mr. Cobb anyway.

I stayed busy the rest of the afternoon until book club started at five thirty. The library had a core group of seven members that read and discussed every book selected. We also had folks we called the dippers. They dipped into a monthly meeting if the book was in their genre of choice. This month's selection was a nonfiction title from Jack Kerouac, *Big Sur*. Our dippers preferred popular fiction, so I knew it would be a smaller group.

I placed the carafe of coffee with some cookies I'd picked up from Nellie Jo on the conference room table. As I arranged the cups and napkins, Tuck Hardesty arrived. He fell in between a core and dipper member. Tuck loved the classics, so I wasn't surprised to see him here for Kerouac. "Good evening, Tuck. Did you finish the book?" I asked.

"Sure did." He showed me a well-worn paperback. "I've read and reread Kerouac since I was a kid. He and Hemingway were my favorites back in high school. Back before you were even alive, Phee." Tuck had been born on the family dairy farm outside Miller's Cove. A lifelong resident, he liked to brag that he found everything he needed in our small town and had no desire to go to the big city.

I pulled my printout of the picture from the newspaper from a manila folder and handed it to him. "Do you recall this band? I'm not sure if they were a local group or from out of town."

Tuck studied the picture. "I sure do. That one right there is Craig Muldean, the fella that used to run the hardware store before his diabetes got so bad. If I recall correctly, one of these guys was from Burlington."

He pointed out Craig to me. If I squinted in the right way, I could see a passing resemblance to the man I knew as Mr. Muldean. The long blonde hair and slim build had given way to a receding crew cut and a pot belly. "Do you know this guy?" I asked, pointing to the man with the belt buckle.

Tuck peered a little closer at the picture. "No, but I'm pretty sure he was the guy from Burlington. To be honest, I was married and just got home from the army when this group got together. I was too busy trying to make a living and take care of a wife and kid. Why do you want to know about a defunct old band?"

I hesitated. If I told Tuck, it would be spread all over town by tomorrow morning. He was also good

13

friends with the sheriff. "I was researching some information about past Founder's Day celebrations and found this. I was curious, that's all."

I was saved from further questioning by the arrival of two more members of the group. I put the picture and the dead body out of my mind for the next hour and went back in time to the sixties and the Beat Generation.

Chapter Four

I locked the doors of the library and decided to walk to Odd Couples. It was a beautiful spring evening, and Clint could drop me back at Velma, my trusty VW van, after dinner.

The diner wasn't busy, and I spotted Clint seated in a corner booth. I was surprised to see Wade sitting at the table with him. "Hey, Wade," I said after I had slid into the seat next to Clint. "Are you and Juliet joining us for dinner?"

"No." He stood and held up a white paper bag with the diner's logo stamped in red on the front. "Takeout for dinner tonight. Juliet has a late yoga class. I was chatting with Clint while I waited for my order."

"Is my sister still freaking out about the wedding?"

Wade ran a hand through his hair, making it stand up in wild angles. "I try to keep in mind that Juliet is a free spirit and prone to different thinking, but she's driving me crazy. My parents are blowing up my phone asking if we've picked a new wedding venue. My grandma's coming down from New York. They haven't met Juliet, so it's hard for me to explain about karma and dead bodies."

I felt his pain. I'd been dealing with Juliet's wild fancies since she was old enough to talk. "I get it. The sooner we can figure out who this dead guy is and solve the crime, the sooner we can get the wedding back on track. I'll talk to her."

"Thanks, Phee. You guys have a good dinner, and I'll see you tomorrow at work."

After Wade left, I turned and gave Clint a quick peck on the lips. I didn't need half the town gossiping about any public displays of affection. I was a librarian, not a spinster from eighteen hundred, but the town had its standards. Librarians were shushers, not smoochers.

"We?" Clint asked.

"We are a couple? We are having dinner?" I wrinkled my forehead.

"You said the sooner *we* can solve the crime. There is no *we* investigation going on, Phee," Clint said, frowning. "Lu told me you were sniffing around this morning looking for information."

"I'm curious, not snooping. It was an educational opportunity to learn how the police investigate cold cases," I said, smiling sweetly.

"Hmm… well, as far as I'm concerned, it's case closed for you and Juliet. Lu's on it, and she's a fine investigator. By the way, she decided not to join us. She's probably scared you'll grill her between dinner and dessert."

I snorted at the thought of Lu being afraid of anyone, but at Clint's baleful look, I held up both my hands in surrender. "I'm off the case. I was simply curious who the guy was. After all, he's been buried in my back yard for forty-plus years. I thought I should at least find out his name."

"No clue. Aside from a few coins and a dollar bill, his wallet contained no identification." He turned towards me and cupped my chin in his hand. "And

16

somehow, you finagled more information from me, my beautiful witchy woman."

"Why, sir, I've done nothing of the sort. I'm just sitting here gasping for a glass of sweet tea," I said in my best imitation of a southern belle. I batted my eyelashes at him.

"Is there something in your eye?"

"Have you never watched *Gone with the Wind* or *Steel Magnolias?*" I knew the answer before I even asked.

"No."

I had been working hard to fill in the gaps in his movie knowledge, but there were still decades of films he had never seen. If he would quit kissing me on my neck the minute the movie started, I might be more successful. I reached into my purse and pulled out a turquoise notebook with a sleepy-eyed sloth on the front. I jotted down a few notes.

Clint chuckled. "What's with the sloth notebook? Is it your version of a cop's notepad?"

"No. I'm bullet journaling."

Clint raised his eyebrows. "When are you around bullets? Not something they checkout at the library as far as I know."

"Ha ha. It's a new thing Willow wants me to try. She said I should journal to release my negative karma. I told her I don't have time, so she suggested a bullet journal. I have a feeling it is just going to be a to do list by the time I'm done."

Clint took a sip of his soda. "I'm intrigued. Can I read it?"

17

"Absolutely not, however, I will tell you that I added more movies to my master list of 'movies Clint needs to watch to be complete.'"

Our waitress, Mindy, came to take our order, so I could be excused for not mentioning that I also wrote down a bullet with Craig Muldean's name. I planned on talking to him tomorrow about the body in my yard.

***

I spent the next morning in my comfortable penguin-themed pajamas with matching slippers. Clint had left earlier and since I had the day off, I planned to catch up on some long overdue cleaning before I went to Mr. Muldean's house to talk to him.

As I washed the morning's dishes, I peered out my window into my backyard. The crime scene tape fluttering in the morning breeze served as a reminder that someone had suffered a terrible fate. I thought about the previous homeowner, seventy-year-old Constance Hammond. She'd lived in the house since 1983 with her husband, Earl. When the upkeep had become too much for them due to Earl's severe arthritis, they sold the property to me and moved into a planned retirement community in Florida. Before the Hammonds, the home sat vacant for three years when the previous homeowner died with no heirs. Had someone taken advantage of the vacant property to rid themselves of a body? If so, it had to be someone local. Who else would know the house was empty?

At ten o'clock, I finished cleaning and dressed

in my favorite jeans and librarian gnome t-shirt. I called Mr. Muldean to see if he was home.

"Come on by. I don't get many visitors these days," Mr. Muldean said.

I decided not to wait, so I grabbed my keys and headed out to interrogate my first possible suspect.

Chapter Five

Craig Muldean lived in a split-level home on the outskirts of town. It had been the start of a subdivision in the late eighties that never lived up to the developer's expectations. The cookie cutter homes lacked the personality of the rest of Miller's Cove. The original plan for a two hundred home community dwindled to a paltry forty-five houses, most of which were rentals.

Velma sputtered to a stop at the curb. I grimaced. Time to take her in for a tune-up and an oil change, but each time I did, the mechanic found something that needed to be replaced. I loved her, but she was an expensive ride to maintain.

Mr. Muldean's lawn had to be the envy of the neighborhood. His grass was a uniform shade of green with a thickness reminiscent of shag carpet. He kept his hedges neatly trimmed and a lovely bed of flowers lined the walk. I rang the doorbell. After two minutes, when no one answered, I knocked. Still no answer. Maybe he had an emergency and left after I talked to him. I knocked one more time and waited. I turned to go back to Velma when I heard a whimper.

"Mr. Muldean?" I put my ear up to the door. There it was again. It sounded like someone was inside. I tried the doorknob. It opened. I peeked my head inside. "Mr. Muldean? It's Phee Jefferson. You and I talked on the phone this morning. Are you okay?"

I wasn't sure, but I thought I heard something. *In for a penny, in for a pound,* as my grandmother used to say. I left the door open and walked into the entryway. A short set of steps led to the kitchen and the living room. I walked up the stairs to the landing. A large painting of the lake hung slightly askew at the top of the landing. The house was decorated nicely inside with quality furniture and tasteful artwork on the walls. It didn't look like the home of a single, older man.

"Mr. Muldean?" I said, but my voice was barely above a whisper. Goosebumps popped up on my arms, despite the warmth. I crept towards the kitchen. I heard another whimper. There, in the middle of the floor, was Mr. Muldean. A Scottish terrier lay next to him, licking his hand.

I dropped to my knees to feel for a pulse. Nothing. It was then that I noticed a pool of blood underneath his head. Craig Muldean was dead. A loud bang from the backyard startled me. I leapt up and ran to the open sliding glass door in the dining area. Looking into the yard, I saw an unlatched gate banging in the wind. My stomach clenched as I realized I probably interrupted the killer. I yanked my phone out of my pocket and called the sheriff's office.

"Sheriff's office," Tammy answered.

"It's Phee Jefferson. You need to send someone to Craig Muldean's house."

"What's going on, Phee? Is he hurt? Do you need an ambulance?" Tammy asked.

"It's too late. He's dead, and I think someone murdered him."

Tammy reassured me that someone would be there as quickly as possible. In the meantime, she told me to wait outside for a deputy to arrive. Miller's Cove is a small town, but it sits in the middle of a rural county. The few deputies we had covered a large area with surrounding farms and holiday homes by the lake. I knew I had at least a few minutes before someone would arrive.

I looked around the kitchen and spotted a full pot of coffee, along with two coffee cups. Had he made coffee in anticipation of my visit or for someone else? I avoided looking at his body and skirted around the counter to the dining area. A shoebox sat on the table. It was full of old letters, newspaper clippings, and photographs. I dug into my purse and pulled out a pen. I used it to flick through the letters, careful not to touch them and leave fingerprints. They were all addressed to someone named Lola Richardson and the post office stamp dated them to the nineties. I couldn't read the postal code. I glanced at the photographs and guessed they were from the late seventies or early eighties based on the clothes.

I pulled out my phone and took pictures of the envelope and a few of the photographs. I gingerly opened one envelope using the tips of my fingers and teased out the letter. Of course, undated. Stuff like that only happened in the movies. I knew someone from the sheriff's office would be here any moment, so I photographed the letter, too. Using the edge of my shirt to protect it from prints, I folded it and maneuvered it back into the envelope.

As I stepped back to head down the steps and wait outside, I spotted a photograph on the floor under the table. I picked it up by the edge and gasped. Just then, I heard a car door slam outside, so I stuffed the photo into a pocket of my purse. I wasn't hiding evidence, not really. I simply thought a photograph of my mother with a man who was not my father draping his arm around her like they were in love applied to the case. Not even if that man was dressed in a pair of bell-bottomed jeans with a belt buckle that matched the one on the dead body in my backyard.

***

I opened the door to find Lu. She didn't look happy to see me. In fact, facing a charging mother bear would be preferable to seeing Lu's face as she pushed her way past me into the house. "Did you touch anything?"

"No, of course–"

She whipped around faster than I thought a pregnant woman should be capable of and eyed me. "Why are you always around when someone shows up dead?"

"Luck?" I shrugged. "I called Mr. Muldean this morning to ask him about a band he used to be connected to. I thought he might tell me who the man buried in my backyard was."

"Why did I bother going to police academy? I could have spent my days reading Nancy Drew and Agatha Marple and saved myself the trouble and the money!"

I winced and was tempted to say Agatha

23

Christie, but I wanted to live to read another day. I chose not to fight the pregnant Lu battle today.

Lu pointed to the door. "Out! I'll come take your statement after I've assessed the scene."

I scurried out the door and sat in Velma. While I waited, I called Juliet.

"Zen Yoga and Meditation. How can I help you find peace today?"

"Juls, I found a dead body."

"Another one? Where? In your front yard? You need a cleansing. I'm calling Willow and the girls."

I waited until she took a breath before I interrupted. "Not at my house. I went to talk to Craig Muldean. He may have had some information to help identify the body. By the time I got here, someone had bashed him over the head in his kitchen."

"Oh, my goddess! Are you okay? Do you need me to come over there? Does Clint know? Do you think the murderer saw you? What do you think he knew that got him killed?"

"Slow down before you hyperventilate and pass out. Lu's here. I need to give my statement before she'll let me leave. As soon as I'm done here, I'll come by the studio. It's important that you see what I found. I'm not sure what to do with it, and I don't want to talk about it on the phone. I'll see you in a little while."

I disconnected before she could ask me anything else. I wondered if I should call Clint and let him know I found another body. Maybe not. That was a conversation that might be better face-to-face. Instead, I sent Clint a text telling him I needed to talk to him. I

24

suggested meeting for a late lunch if he wasn't on patrol. For the next five minutes, I stared at the screen, waiting for a response. In a small community like Miller's Cove, I doubted I would be the first person to tell him I had found another body. Chances were, Tammy called him right after she had dispatched Lu to the scene.

A sharp rap on my window made me squeal. Lu stood glowering outside my car window. I sighed. I really preferred a bear. Even a hungry grizzly would be safer.

Forty-five minutes later, I pulled into the small parking lot next to Juliet's new studio. An old Victorian house with the downstairs originally gutted five years ago to make a vegan bakery and coffee house. It encompassed the cozy spirit of Miller's Cove. The bakery business had folded within a year, and the building stood vacant until Juliet convinced the owner to rent her the entire place. She converted the downstairs into her yoga studio and lived in the rooms upstairs.

I entered the studio and sat quietly in the corner while Juliet finished leading a class of seniors through chair yoga. My foot jiggled, and it took every ounce of my willpower not to pace the floor. *What was Mom doing with the dead guy?* This thought led to a dozen more unanswered questions. *How come I know nothing about Mom's boyfriends before she met Dad at university? Did Dad know this man? Did Dad kill this man in a fit of jealousy?*

So consumed with my thoughts, I didn't realize

the class was over until Mrs. Lancaster touched me on my arm. "Hello, Phee. I haven't had a chance to see you in a few days. You need to pop next door for a cup of tea. Lots of goings on over at your house."

It was a question, but Mrs. Lancaster tended to speak in imperatives rather than requests. She was a wonderful neighbor, and I felt a twinge of guilt that I hadn't stopped by to see her.

"Yes, ma'am. I'll stop by this afternoon. I have a few things I need to take care of, but I should be home no later than three."

"I'll see you at three-thirty then." She nodded goodbye.

"What is going on?" Juliet hissed as the last of her seniors left the studio. "I leave you alone for a day, and you find another body. You should have gone to work for the sheriff rather than the library."

Without a word, I whipped the photograph of Mom and the man who was not our father and thrust it at her. I tapped my foot, waiting for a reaction.

"Yeah," Juliet said. "Mom is leaning against the car with some hot guy except for the ridiculous mustache. You realize our mother had a life before us, right?"

"I know that, smarty pants. Look closer at the picture of the guy. Do you see anything that may have sparked my interest? Somewhere in the pants region, maybe?"

"Things that bad between you and Clint already?" Juliet snickered at me.

"Grow up. Look at the belt buckle. Is it

familiar?"

She took the photograph out of my hands. "Maybe. I mean, it isn't the clearest picture, and it's not like there's a close-up shot of the buckle. You know who we need to help us? Willow."

I arched a brow. "Willow? What's she going to do? Consult her spirit guides?"

Juliet waved my sarcasm aside with her hand. "You mock me, but maybe she can reach out to our victims."

I shook my head. "Good luck with that." I needed to see Clint and explain about today. "I need to go see my boyfriend about a body."

She gave me a sympathetic look. Juliet knew Clint and how he would react. "Poor Mr. Muldean. I loved going to the hardware store when I was a kid. Remember those lollies he gave us?"

A memory of Mr. Muldean with his thick shock of silver hair leaning over the counter to hand us a lollie flashed through my mind. I took a deep breath to stop the threat of tears. "He was such a nice man. I wondered what he knew that made someone kill him?"

"Do you really think it's related to our John Doe?" Juliet asked.

"I don't know, but it is odd someone killed him after we found the body and right after I called him."

Juliet gave me a hug. "Be careful, Flea. I don't want to live without my weird sister. Perhaps you should sit out this investigation and leave it to Clint. A person is a pretty nasty character to murder sweet, old Mr. Muldean."

"Don't worry. I promised Clint I would stick to historical research from now on, and that's exactly what I plan to do. I need to go if I'm going to catch Clint at the station for lunch. Come by the house this evening for a glass of wine and bring the photograph. We need to come up with a game plan to confront Mom."

"We ask."

"Ask?"

"Yes, ask. We ask our mother who the man in the photograph is. It's Mom, not a hardened criminal we need to interrogate."

"If you say so. We'll do it when Dad's at the university. No need to bring up the ghosts of boyfriends past when he's around."

"Are you really my sister?" Juliet asked. "Seriously? Dad had girlfriends before Mom. Mom had boyfriends before Dad. It's life. Get over it."

I gave her my best duck face and said goodbye. I would have to hustle if I was going to make it to lunch. I just hoped the hard knot forming in my stomach when I thought of telling Clint about Mr. Muldean would go away before I saw him.

Chapter Six

When I pulled into the parking lot, I saw Clint leaning against his patrol car. I took a moment to admire his lean physique and how sexy he looked in his khaki uniform. Then I tried to ignore the scowl that graced his handsome face.

I hopped out of Velma and appeared nonchalant as I walked over to him and gave him a peck on the lips. He grabbed me and pulled me into a tight hug.

"They could have killed you," Clint whispered, then he gave me a rough kiss that left me a little breathless. After he finished ravishing my lips like a hero from a 1940s movie, he held me at arm's length. "Find no more bodies, do you hear me?"

"It's not like I go looking for them," I protested. "I only wanted a nice wedding for my sister, and now it's all gone to hell in a handbasket."

"Why were you going to see Craig Muldean?" Clint asked.

"I'll tell you, but let's grab some lunch. It's easier to explain when I show you what I discovered in the newspaper archives. Plus, we're giving Mr. Meacham a show." I nodded my head towards the insurance office where Clyde Meacham stood watching us from his window. I felt judged.

Clint put his arm around me and led me back to Velma. "I'll follow you. I'm patrolling the far side of the county this afternoon and need to head that way after we eat."

I drove to the new sandwich shop that recently

29

opened called The Bread Heads. A middle-aged couple who owned a summer cottage had retired from their corporate jobs and live in Miller's Cove full-time. They shared a passion for deli meats and customer service. They quickly became a favorite lunch spot for a lot of locals.

We placed our orders and waited at a small table for our number to be called. It was after their big lunch rush, so we had the place to ourselves except for a young couple who couldn't stop holding hands and giggling at a corner table.

"Tell me what happened with Craig Muldean and leave nothing out." Clint demanded.

"First, let me show you something." I pulled the printout from the newspaper about The Screaming Goats performing at the Founder's Day celebration in 1979 and handed it to him. "Notice the guy with the gaudy belt buckle. It's exactly like the one the guy in the grave was wearing. I don't know about you, but I can't see this being a factory-made buckle everyone owned. That buckle makes a statement."

Clint said nothing. He scratched his chin and looked closely at the photograph. "Maybe. We found a maker's mark on it. Someone handcrafted it. It still doesn't explain why you went to talk to Mr. Muldean rather than sharing this information with, perhaps, the love of your life, who is also a sheriff's deputy."

I took a sip of my soda to give myself a moment to think about how to respond. "I didn't want to bother you if it turned out to be a dead end. The photograph in the newspaper is almost forty years old. It seemed like a long shot."

"Your long shot seems like it was pretty darn accurate. How does Mr. Muldean tie into your newspaper clipping?"

"He was a member of the band." I pointed to the younger version of Craig. "It means he also knew who our John Doe was."

"My John Doe. Not our John Doe. You, librarian." Clint pointed at me. "Me, deputy sheriff, and actually trained to investigate crime."

"Okay, Tarzan. Point taken. Regardless, admit that I might be onto something. Can you at least give what I've found to Lu?"

"I will." Clint took a sip of his soda. He folded the picture and then tucked it into his shirt pocket. "If, and it is a big if since there's no guarantee we can tie the skeleton in your yard to Craig's murder. If the two cases are related, then whoever is behind it is a dangerous individual. Killing Craig in such a violent manner…"

Clint didn't finish what he was going to say because, at that moment, my mother came into the sandwich shop and called out my name.

"Hi, Mom," I responded when she had made her way to our table. She squeezed in next to me. "You don't have classes today?"

"It's spring break. Your father and I were going to spend the week camping in the mountains, but we decided after the incident to stick close to home." She used air quotes around the word incident.

"Incident?" I raised my eyebrow. I considered

interrogating my mother about the man who had his arm around her in the photograph, but I knew my meddling in the investigation wouldn't thrill Clint. Plus, I tampered with potential evidence. Sometimes I acted before I thought things through.

"Your sister should get married in the church. No dead bodies. No red tide. A simple ceremony in a safe place. I try to stay out of your love lives, but it's silly to believe that some invisible entity is sending a message that the marriage is doomed." She blew a stray hair out of her eyes.

I could tell Juliet's phobia about the wedding exasperated my mother because she drummed her fingers on the table. My mother loathed fidgety people. "I'm working on her, Mom. If Lu solves the case, maybe Juliet will settle down and agree to still have the ceremony at my house."

"No pressure," Clint grumbled, but a hint of a smile offset his growl.

"Speaking of pressure, how are you two doing?" Mom asked.

Her words were innocent, but the underlying message was clear. When was Clint going to marry me and give her a grandchild? My brother and his wife have twins which I had hoped would buy Juliet and I more time before our mother's attention turned towards us, but clearly not.

"We're fine, Mother." I hope the use of mother rather than the usual mom gave her a hint. Clint and I *were* doing well. We had talked about getting married, but we both were hesitant. I knew why he was leery.

His parents' marriage had been a disaster. I wasn't so sure why I wasn't quite ready to commit to Clint forever.

"Hm…" She turned and looked over the chalkboard menu. "I think I'll stick to the Dilly Cheese Melt. So far, it's my favorite." She went to the counter to place her order.

While she was gone, the server delivered our sandwiches. I took a huge bite of my roast beef and cheddar sandwich with its huge slathering of a special horseradish sauce that I swore I would need to learn to duplicate. My mother nattered on about her students at the university where she taught, which saved us from further interrogation about our love life.

Clint finished his sandwich, then took his last few fries and added them to my pile. "I've got to get back to work. I'll see you at home. Mrs. Jefferson, good to see you."

He gave me a quick peck and was out the door. The server delivered Mom's sandwich, so she slid her plate over to his empty spot and moved to the bench opposite of me. "What's going on with the investigation? I know you know something. We have got to get your sister's wedding back on track."

"They are still trying to identify the body, but you might help with that."

"Me? What would I know about a dead man buried in your backyard? I swear, Phee, reading all those mysteries might have turned your brain to mush. You should stick to the classics."

I pulled the picture I had taken from Craig

33

Muldean out of my purse and slid it across the table to her.

"Is this you?" I pointed to the young woman in the photo.

My mother picked it up and let out a small gasp of delight. "Oh, my word! Yes, it is me. Look at my hair. It was my literal crowning glory. The hours I spent straightening." She shook her head. "Where did you find this? Did you go rummaging through my photo albums?"

I shook my head but didn't elaborate. I didn't want to tell her that I stole it from an active crime scene. "I found it. How well did you know the guy in this picture and Craig Muldean?"

"Craig? Why are you asking about him?"

"Mom, someone murdered Craig today right before I arrived at his house." I waited for the eruption, but her shock at my news still rolled over me in waves.

"What? When? Why were you at Craig's? What in the world is happening in Miller's Cove?" My mother's voice had risen in pitch and volume, and a few of the people at nearby tables turned to look at us.

"Mom, not so loudly! I discovered him this morning when I went to visit him to ask him about the guy in my grave." I told her everything that happened at Craig's. "This guy's belt buckle matches the dead man's."

My mother stared at the photograph. When she looked back up at me, tears glistened. "Dean. His name was Dean Winters. I thought he ran off to California. That's all he talked about that summer."

"When did he disappear?"

She was silent for a few minutes. "I suppose it was 1979. It was the summer before I left for college and before I met your father. Dean was a summer fling. He had moved to from Burlington to Miller's Cove during my senior year. He was older and joined a band that played locally. I thought he was the hottest thing since the invention of the toaster."

"Do you remember the last time you saw him?"

Mom sniffled and gave me a watery smile. "I do. It was on Founder's Day. They performed at the picnic. We had an ugly argument, and I left and went home. I didn't see him again."

I gulped. I didn't want to say it, but Mom arguing with Dean Winters right before he went missing made her a suspect in his murder. Now I wished I hadn't gone snooping.

Chapter Seven

I remained silent while I thought about how to ask my mom the next question without interrogating her. "It must have been tough to have him leave without a word," I said. "I can't imagine how I would have reacted when I was a teenager. Probably wailing and gnashing of teeth with a ton of ice cream involved."

My mother smiled. "You've always been the dramatic one in the family."

"Me? Juliet thinks invisible spirits are out to ruin her wedding, and I'm the dramatic one?"

Mom waved my comment aside. "Juliet's quirky, but you've always had the flair for the dramatic in your love life. Remember when that blonde-haired boy… what was his name?"

"Ron," I said, drily. "His name was Ron, and I had good reason to be upset. He asked my best friend to the prom, even though he and I had gone on a date the weekend before. Who does that?"

"You cried all weekend and swore you would never love again. I think you watched *An Affair to Remember* ten times in two days."

I rolled my eyes. I couldn't believe that my family thought I was dramatic, but I had more important things to worry about, like verifying the dead guy was Dean Winters and what my mom remembered about him.

"Do you recall what you and Dean argued about that day?" I asked, trying to refocus the conversation on my current problem.

36

Mom thought for a moment. "Honestly, it was pretty silly. Frank Matthews had asked me for a date earlier that day. I told Dean, and he threatened to slug Frank the next time he saw him. I thought he was being a typical macho man and acting like I couldn't handle things myself."

"Frank Matthews? Our former county director of finance? What does he do now? Something with real estate, I think." I pushed my lunch plate aside with regret. I didn't need to eat those last few fries if I was going to fit into a bridesmaid's dress.

"Yes. He's a real estate developer now. He and I went to high school together. He was always on the fringes of the crowd. You know the type, not unpopular, but never the center of attention. The argument about Frank led to him pushing me to go to California." She stopped talking and looked thoughtful. "Maybe I'm remembering wrong. Honestly, it's forty years ago. I could be wrong."

"Can you think of anyone who would have wanted to hurt Dean?" I asked.

My mother narrowed her eyes. "You aren't sticking your nose into this investigation, are you? You need to leave well enough alone. Look what happened to Craig?" She grabbed my hands. "It could have been you with your head bashed in. Let it go, Phee."

I extricated my hands from her grip. "It's fine, Mom. I'm not sticking my nose anywhere other than the newspaper archives. I've told Clint everything I know." Everything except that my mom knew the victim.

We finished our lunch. I promised her that Clint and I would come for dinner on Sunday. She left to finish her errands, and I went to Willow's place to see if she could help me find a new location for Juliet's wedding that would please the spirit guides without being ridiculously expensive to book.

I had to drive past Craig Muldean's house to get to Willow's. I slowed Velma down as I passed by the crime scene tape across his driveway. Poor Mr. Muldean. Whatever he knew got him killed, and I could only assume Dean Winters' death played a role.

I took the road to the lake. Willow had become a year-long resident after the previous summer. She now ran a web-based psychic counseling business from her cottage. She also dabbled in painting, jewelry making, and had recently taken up welding with a plan to construct large sculptures. I limited my artistic talents to adult coloring books. I recently started an adult coloring night at the library, and it surprised me with the number and diversity of people who attended.

I pulled up to Willow's cottage. I loved the whimsical nature of her yard. She had several gnomes peeking out from behind butterfly bushes and patches of coneflowers. The small tree in her yard had a Celtic Green Man attached, and if you peered close enough at the dogwood, you could see a tiny fairy door at its base.

The sound of hammering greeted me. I followed the noise to the backyard. Willow was in the oak tree hammering some pieces of wood.

I squinted my eyes against the early afternoon sun. "What are you building?"

Willow paused her enthusiastic banging and wiped the sweat from her forehead. "A treehouse."

"What for?" It was always dangerous to ask the reasoning behind Willow's activities, but I felt adventurous.

She set down her hammer and climbed to the ground. She picked up a mason jar of tea from its resting spot on the ground and took a big drink before answering. "I want to feel closer to nature when I meditate, but I also don't want to get soaking wet when it rains or snows, so a treehouse."

I couldn't fault her logic, although I wondered if it might be a little dangerous climbing a tree when it was icy and snowing.

"Come on inside. I need to take a break anyway. All this sawing and hammering has made me hungry. Have you eaten? I have a phenomenal couscous mixed with some wild-picked greens."

I shuddered at the description. I loved couscous as much as the next girl, but Willow added ingredients that were good for you rather than tasty.

"I've eaten, thanks. Actually, I wanted to see if you knew where we could hold the wedding that would please the spirit guides. I know Juliet said she wanted to cancel everything, but I think if we found someplace cosmically pleasing, she might change her mind."

Willow opened her refrigerator and took out a stoneware bowl. I made the mistake of glancing at it when she set it on the counter. It was a mishmash of couscous, bits of dandelion, and a few suspicious pieces of mushrooms and green leaves. She scooped out a healthy serving onto a plate and motioned for me to sit down.

"I think anyplace would do," Willow said. "The problem isn't the location, it's you."

My eyes widened. "Me? What in the world are you talking about?"

Willow closed her eyes and stayed silent for several minutes. If I didn't know how she and her spirit guides operated, I would have assumed she had fallen asleep, but it was how she talked with them. I don't know if I believed she communicated with the dearly departed, but I couldn't argue with her results.

Willow opened her eyes and nodded her head. "As I suspected, you are resistant to the idea of happily ever after. You created negative energy around the wedding, and it's causing disruption in the universe."

"Are you kidding me? I'm the queen of happy endings. I make Cinderella and her prince look like a B-Movie. Your spirit guides are wrong." As far as I was concerned, Willow's spirit guides picked the wrong person. I needed to set the record straight.

"Are you really?" Willow whispered. "My guides are never wrong."

"I know every scene in every old romantic movie. I cry at weddings. For Pete's sake, I watch the Hallmark movie channel." I crossed my arms. "I'm the most romantically inclined person I know."

"In fiction, perhaps, but how about in real life?" Willow stood and walked over to a row of shelves that contained all her dried herbs and whatnots she used to help her clients. She opened jars and pinch out different herbs into a small ceramic bowl.

"I love Clint," I said, "and I want to be with him. He's always been the one."

Willow stopped mixing her herbs and turned to look at me, her gaze so intense it made me look away. "I don't doubt you love Clint, but do you believe deep inside that he truly loves you? Isn't there something always niggling away at the back of your mind that is waiting for him to walk away?"

I opened my mouth to protest but stopped and considered what she said. "I'm realistic with my relationship expectations," I protested, but my words sounded weak even to me.

She turned back to her herbs and whispered something under her breath as she put a final pinch of something purple into her concoction. When she was done, she gently poured the mixture into a small cloth bag and tied it closed with twine. She handed it to me.

"Put this under your pillow. It will help," she said. "I'm not a relationship expert. As you can see, I live alone, but if you always expect the proverbial other shoe to drop, then you always have one foot out the door in the relationship."

I knew she was probably right, but I didn't want to face that part of myself. There was a grave in my backyard and a murder that needed to be solved. I would wait until after I had solved those crimes to lie on a therapist's couch to excavate my emotions. "Listen, I could spend weeks picking apart my emotional health and wellbeing, but right now, I need to solve the immediate problem in my life. Two dead bodies in less than a week."

"Two?"

I told Willow all about Craig and what had happened. When I finished, she closed her eyes again.

"What do the spirit guides have to say?" I asked.

"I wasn't talking to them. I said a small prayer that Craig would find peace. He seemed kind, but I knew him only in passing."

"He was." I got up to leave. "Will you please help get this wedding on track? Tell the spirit guides I'll work on myself when the wedding is over."

"I'll see what I can do. Be careful, Phee. I sense someone has secrets that could harm more than one person in Miller's Cove, and they'll do anything to keep them hidden."

Chapter Eight

I left Willow's house in a dour mood. I was so lost in thought that I almost drove past my street. As I guided Velma towards my home, I saw a car with an out-of-state license plate parked in front of my house.

When I pulled into my driveway, the car door opened, and Anthony stepped out. My heart sank. Not that I was unhappy to see Anthony, but I dreaded lying to him. Lu had sworn us all to secrecy under penalty of her locking us in a jail cell. Anthony didn't know that she was pregnant with his child. We didn't understand her convoluted reasoning, but she was our friend. There was no way in a town as small as Miller's Cove that he wouldn't run into her or find out.

I pulled out my phone and texted Juliet to tell her that Anthony was at my house. Once that was done, I plastered a big smile on my face and got out to greet him. "Hey there, stranger!" I gave him a quick hug. "What brings you back to Miller's Cove?"

"Taking a break from the campaign trail to visit my favorite librarian. And try to talk some sense into Lu. I'm at a loss for why she left me. It's tearing me apart. I thought if I gave her some space, she would change her mind, but it's been months and not a word."

I saw his face looked tired, and he had lost some weight. Anthony Ziegfried usually exuded confidence and success. He possessed the polished good looks of an Ivy League education. He had red hair like me, but he kept his cut close and straight, while mine was a wild mass of curls I fought to control daily. His bright

43

blue eyes usually gleamed with intelligence behind
stylish frames, but today, they just looked sad and tired.

I sighed. Lu was going to kill me, but Anthony
was my friend, too. In fact, he saved my life when
Juliet and I investigated the murder of Senator
Campbell's daughter two years ago. "Come inside. We
need to talk."

I unlocked the door. Watson and Fritz barked
like crazy creatures until they realized Anthony was
someone they knew. As usual, Ferdinand, my Maine
Coon Cat, ignored everyone. Anthony followed me to
the kitchen. I grabbed a bottle of red wine that I had
bought the day before and two glasses. I poured us both
a glass before sitting down next to him.

Anthony looked at the glass of wine. "It's not
even five o'clock. Is it really that bad? Has Lu found
someone else? I'll win her back."

I grabbed his hand to stop him. "It's not a new
man." I am never at a loss for words. My brother
swears I even talked in my sleep as a child because I
had so much to say, but in this moment, I didn't know
how to tell Anthony about Lu and the baby. I took a big
gulp of wine. "It isn't my place to tell you what's going
on with Lu. I don't understand what's going on inside
of her brain, but I know she loves you. She's just
contrary."

Anthony ran his hand through his hair, making
it stand on end. He resembled an older Opie from
Mayberry. "You're right. I love her so damn much it's
killing me to be away from her. I'll do anything to win
her back. If I only knew why she left me to begin with,

I could change it."

"It's not anything you did," I said. "Well, you did something, but you didn't. Ugh! I wish I could tell you, but I can't break this kind of news to you. Promise me one thing."

"If it will help me with Lu, I promise."

"Promise me when you see her, you'll be patient. She's got something going on inside of her head." *And her body.*

"You can't tell me?" Anthony asked, his eyes pleading. "Throw me a bone, Phee. I've got two days before I need to get back to the senator. I'm working on something here, but I'm not ready to share."

I wanted to tell him. I wanted to tell him to run, not walk, to Lu and shake her into letting him back into her life and their soon-to-be-born child's life. Anthony and Lu deserved a happily ever after. Instead, I shook my head.

"I'm sorry, Anthony. I promised Lu I wouldn't say anything. You're my friend, too, but she carries a gun. You know she'll use it."

Anthony blew out a breath and picked up his glass of wine. He drained the glass, then poured himself another. "I understand, but I don't like it. I admire your loyalty, so I'll have to figure it out on my own."

"It will all work out in the end. I know it." I hoped I sounded more confident than I felt. Lu's moods and emotions had always been mercurial, but with the hormones of pregnancy coursing through her, who knows how she would react to Anthony's sudden reappearance?

The two of us sat silently drinking our wine, each lost in our own thoughts. I was considering how to find out more information about Dean Winters. With a library board meeting in the morning, I needed to prepare for, I should have some quiet time to go through more newspaper archives in the afternoon. I was so absorbed in my mental checklist that I didn't hear the front door open.

"Hey, Anthony! Good to see you," Clint said, startling me out of my revelry.

Anthony stood and shook Clint's hand. "Good to see you. How are things?"

Clint removed his hat and dropped it on the table. "Busy. It got even busier after Phee found another body today. Sheriff swears it's going to kill the tourist trade this summer, no pun intended."

Anthony gave him a quizzical look. "Another dead body?" He turned to me. "Why didn't you say something? Are you poking around in a murder investigation again?"

I waved his question aside. "You have more important things on your mind."

"A new baby is definitely more important," Clint said.

Anthony's eyes widened. "Baby? What the hell are you talking about, Clint? What new baby?"

Oh, sugar. Lu was going to kill us. I shot Clint a murderous look.

He grimaced, then laid a hand on Anthony's shoulder. "Sit back down."

Anthony dropped into the chair like a puppet

whose strings suddenly snapped. He picked up his wineglass and saw that it was empty.

Clint took it from his hand. "I think this conversation calls for something a little stronger."

Chapter Nine

The next morning, I hit the snooze button three times before rolling out of bed. Clint had left an hour previously for work, and I usually woke up with him to drink our coffee together. Although my heart was in it, my body had protested too much. The body won the round. My head ached and when I glanced in the mirror on my way to retrieve a cup of coffee, I saw my face swollen like a marshmallow mascot.

Anthony had slept in our guest room last night, and when I peeked in the open door, he was still passed out cold. It had taken all of Clint's considerable strength and my voice of reason to keep Anthony from charging over to Lu's last night. I explained to him that Lu must have had a good reason to keep the news that she was pregnant with his child to herself. If he acted like a rabid dog by attacking her and demanding an immediate explanation, she would clam up. After an hour of whiskey, wine, and loud shouting from him and us, he finally conceded that we were right.

I poured coffee into my biggest mug and added a generous splash of cream. Clint and I occasionally enjoyed a glass or two of wine or beer after work or with friends, but both of us gave up drinking copious amounts of alcohol when we left college. I would pay dearly for last night as I sat through what promised to be a long board meeting at nine o'clock.

An hour later, I was in the meeting room waiting for the board members to arrive. I had left Anthony a note next to a fresh pot of coffee and told him to help himself. I prayed he would use wisdom and patience today when he looked for Lu.

At five minutes to nine, Wade opened the door to the library to allow the board members inside. We didn't open until nine, but the four men and three women liked to arrive early so the meeting could start on time. My neighbor, Mrs. Lancaster, was board president.

An older man with a haircut that belonged to a six-year-old boy rather than an adult was the last to arrive. He was our newest board member. I hadn't met him, but his face seemed vaguely familiar. I must have passed him inside the grocery store or at Nellie Jo's coffee shop. He came dressed for business in a suit and tie, but he wore loafers with no socks, which immediately set off my gross alarm.

"I'm Ophelia Jefferson," I said, extending my hand to shake his. "It's a pleasure to meet you and thank you for agreeing to serve on the library board."

"Graham Lawson. Nice to meet you." He ignored my outstretched hand. Although he smiled at me, disapproval radiated from every inch of him. It was an unfamiliar feeling for me from the board members.

I indicated a seat at the large conference table to him. I picked up the sheets of paper with the agenda I had copied earlier and passed them around before taking a seat myself at one end.

"I'd like to call this meeting to order," Mrs. Lancaster said. "Before we get into library business, I want to extend a warm welcome to our newest member, Graham Lawson."

49

AMY E. LILLY

"Thank you. It's a pleasure to be back in Miller's Cove. I'm looking forward to taking an active role in the community. The library's as good a place to start as any."

With that glowing endorsement ringing in my ears, Mrs. Lancaster began the meeting.

***

Two hours later, my head pounded, and I said a small prayer to Willow's spirit guide that someone would pull the fire alarm so the meeting would end.

"I don't see why new bookshelves should cost so much," Mr. Falcone protested. "The kids in the high school shop class could build you shelves for just the cost of a few sheets of plywood, some two-by-fours and some wood stain."

I clenched my hands together to keep from jumping across the table and shaking him. "As I explained, Mr. Falcone, with metal library shelving, they will last long after you and I are gone, and they are adjustable. We're not someone's private home library. Homemade bookshelves won't do the job."

Mr. Falcone looked like he wanted to say something else, but Mrs. Shires stopped him. "Tony, I understand you have reservations about spending money. It's what makes you a good treasurer, but you are looking to save pennies where we needn't save them. We are trying to move Miller's Cove into the twenty-first century, not roll it back to the nineteen fifties with kids from shop class building our shelves. I move we approve the money and be done with it."

50

Mrs. Lancaster sized the chance. "We have a motion on the table. All those in favor, say, aye."

I heard a chorus of ayes with a final begrudging one from Tony Falcone. The meeting finally adjourned. I got up from my chair, ready to dash to my office to find some aspirin stashed in my desk. I was almost at the door when Graham Lawson blocked my escape.

"Might I have a quick word with you, Miss–it is Miss, isn't it–Miss Jefferson?" It was a statement rather than a request, but I stepped back into the room to allow others to move past us.

"Of course. What can I help you with?"

Graham waited until the last board member left, then quietly closed the door. The false smile he had worn during the meeting was now gone.

"I have some concerns about some of your activities in the community," he said. "I didn't want to bring them up at my first meeting, so I kept them to myself for now."

The "*for now*" was an obvious threat that he could change his mind. I remained silent. I wondered which community activities sparked his concern–my reading to the seniors at Shady Pines, pet food for fines campaign to help the shelter, or was it my work with the local businesses to pick up litter once a month on the road to the lake and tourist cottages? Environmental concerns were quite subversive.

When I failed to respond, Graham continued. "I'm sure I don't need to remind you, but you're the public face of the library. When you choose to make poor choices outside of these walls, it unfortunately reflects on the institution."

"And what poor choices, in your view, have I made?" I tried to keep the venom in my voice to a minimum, but I could feel my temper rising.

Graham clucked his tongue. "Not just my view, I'm sure, but others in the community are concerned that you find yourself increasingly embroiled in crime. It's unseemly."

I clenched my fists tightly, then relaxed them. It wouldn't do for me to lose my cool. *It takes all kinds to make up this world,* I reminded myself. Even pompous men with poor taste in footwear deserved a spot on the board.

"I certainly didn't ask to have a body buried in my backyard, Mr. Lawson," I said. "I've only owned the house for three years. The murder in question happened before I was even born. Surely you don't believe that I could have had anything to do with it. After all, time travel isn't possible. Not yet anyway." I gave him my best hundred-dollar smile while inside my stomach churned from too much wine the night before and too little sleep. I reached for the door handle and prayed there was aspirin in my desk drawer.

Mr. Lawson laid his hand on my arm to restrain me. "I'm talking about the murder of Craig Muldean. Miss Jefferson, surely you realize it appears suspicious that you were on the scene of a murder just days after the discovery of a corpse in your backyard. I'm simply saying what the rest of the town is thinking."

I looked pointedly at his hand on my arm. He released me and stepped back. "Thank you for your concern, Mr. Lawson. Now if you'll excuse me, I need to focus on running the library. Have a good day."

I stalked out of the room, not caring that the red patent leather pumps I wore for the meeting made a racket. Startled, Wade looked up from his computer and gave me a questioning look. I held my hand up and strode past him. When I dropped into my chair, it flung around in a circle and almost took me out. I grabbed the desk edge to steady myself and closed my eyes. "He's a toad. He's a toad. Do not let him get to you. You're a good librarian. A great librarian, in fact." I said under my breath.

"You're an outstanding librarian," Wade said from the doorway.

I peered through the glass window of my office and saw the doors of the library closing behind the blue-suited back of Mr. Graham Lawson. "Our new board member thinks I'm unseemly," I said. I rummaged around in my top desk drawer and pulled out a bottle of aspirin.

"Well, there was that time you and Juliet donned matching bedazzled ski masks. As a fashion statement, even in my humble male opinion, it was rather unseemly," Wade joked.

I slammed my desk drawer shut. "Who does he think he is? The morality police?"

"He's the preacher of the new church on the outskirts of town. You know, the enormous one that looks more like a museum or office building than a church."

"Aren't they the ones that make it mandatory to

let them access your bank account to insure you're tithing ten percent?" I asked.

They began construction on the new church in the past year to accommodate the growing population of Miller's Cove. We were still a small town, but as Burlington became larger, families were fleeing the city for a more rural setting. I had driven past the construction site a few times, but I was loyal to our Miller's Cove Community Church and Reverend Taylor. My parents attended every Sunday, and Clint and I joined them at least once a month.

"It is. Graham Lawson plans to expand his ministry to a weekly television show. He approached my friend who works at WVCR out of Burlington," Wade said. "For now, they are holding services in the high school auditorium."

"Why Miller's Cover? It seems an odd location to build an uber ministry."

"I bet your mom knows him. He grew up in Miller's Cove before he moved to Kansas. Or was it Nebraska? It doesn't matter. It was a flat state. He and his wife built a huge new house on the lake, too. It's all glass and steel. Does not blend with the woods at all," Wade said.

I took a swallow of water from my water bottle– my environmentally friendly water bottle made of recycled glass–and decided I would attend church this Sunday. I could ask Reverend Taylor what he knew about the new preacher in town and talk to my mother to see what she might remember about him. He would be my board member for the next two years. Any

54

insight into Graham Lawson's personality might help me get off his bad side.

In the meantime, I had a library to run and books to catalog. If only my mind would stop gnawing away at why Graham Lawson's face looked so familiar.

Chapter Ten

After the uncomfortable meeting with Graham Lawson, I turned my focus to the library. It wasn't difficult. The annual Founder's Day celebration was only two months away, and I kept busy measuring space and getting quotes from vendors for my new shelves. I would leave the detecting to the detectives, I decided.

I left the library with a sense of accomplishment. I had contacted several volunteers who would assist staff in moving the books from the old shelves to the new when they arrived, and I had organized the summer reading supplies. With such a small staff–Wade and I were the only full-timers–I juggled many jobs within the library. There were times I had considered moving to a larger library system in Burlington, but I enjoyed the variety and knew I wouldn't have that in a larger library.

I had invited Anthony to stay with us tonight rather than an impersonal hotel, so I stopped at the grocery store on the way home and picked up supplies for fajitas. Wade and Juliet were coming over, too, since they both wanted to see him.

Clint's truck was in the driveway when I arrived home. His hours varied, so we didn't often get to spend an evening together with friends. I found him sitting on the back porch watching Watson and Fritz play tug-of-war with one of their toys. Ferdie sat on the railing, his tail twitching as he watched his frenemies.

I settled down in the chair next to him with my

glass of Chardonnay and felt the day's worries fade. "Rough day?" I asked him.

Clint took a swallow of his beer. "You could say that. There was a nasty accident outside of town. Older folks just passing through the area swerved to miss a deer and ended up rolling their car."

"My goodness! Are they okay?"

I couldn't imagine seeing what Clint saw regularly. Although we had a fairly low crime rate, he saw everything from car accidents to domestic abuse. Most people were decent, but just like everywhere else, we had our share of problems.

"Eventually. It was bad. The wife was in critical condition, and the husband kept saying it was all his fault and he wouldn't forgive himself." He shook his head. "It was sad."

I reached over and held his hand. We sat in silence, watching the boys play. It felt right being here with him, sharing our thoughts, building a life. Willow's spirit guides were things of stuff and nonsense.

"Did Anthony go to the station to find Lu?" I asked.

"I don't think so. She was busy talking to the crime scene people about Craig's murder and pursuing the information you gave me about The Screaming Goats. If he had shown up at the station, she wouldn't have been as pleasant as she was."

I laughed. He was right. A fiery combination of her father's Irish cop heritage and her Puerto Rican mother, Lu was not one to mince words with her feelings or her opinion. She was my friend, but she was scary sometimes.

"Well, we have a full table tonight. Anthony, Wade, and Juliet will be here, and I need to get supper started or we'll be ordering a pizza." I stood up and stretched.

Clint stood and whistled for the dogs. "I'll help. My spaghetti noodles are all the rage in Italy."

I kissed him and snuggled against his chest. "I've heard that it's a hard task to master boiling the water. Every time you get it right, I am so impressed."

He pulled me closer. "That's not all I get right." He growled against my neck and nibbled my ear.

I gave him a playful push. I didn't dare respond, or we would have to order takeout for everyone. A sharp knock on the front door followed by Anthony's voice shouting hello stopped any chance of Clint's unspoken promise being fulfilled.

"We're back here," I yelled, and pulled open the screen door.

Anthony strolled into the kitchen with an enormous bag from Maybe Baby boutique. Valerie Clark, the owner, had been Clint's girlfriend in high school. I had spent years disliking her out of jealousy and insecurity, but the two of us had talked, and I discovered she was a nice person with troubles and insecurities of her own. I visited her store all the time to buy baby clothes and toys for my twin niece and nephew.

Clint raised an eyebrow at the bag. "Been shopping?"

"I went shopping for my future son and/or daughter. Is she having twins? I glimpsed her leaving the police station. She's huge," Anthony said, concern apparent on his face.

"Not that I know. I'm sure she would have mentioned if she was. Did you talk to her?" I asked.

"Not yet. I have a plan guaranteed to work, and I'd appreciate it if you two wouldn't say anything to her. I'm keeping a low profile until I have it all in place."

"She won't hear anything from me, man," Clint said. "You want a beer?"

"Why don't you two go into the den? I work better without testosterone under my feet," I said.

Clint was wonderful to have around the house to fix broken sinks or paint trim, but he was a hot mess in the kitchen. I ended up spending more time cleaning up after him when he "helped" cook than if I had done it myself. I appreciated his thoughtfulness, if not the actual action.

"Are you sure?" Clint asked.

I shooed the two of them out of the way and got busy chopping green peppers, onions, and garlic for my sauce.

"Hello? The fun couple is here!" Juliet called from the front hallway. "And we brought wine and dessert."

Juliet and Wade came into the kitchen. Wade carried an impressive-looking cheesecake while Juliet presented me with a bottle of red wine. "Where are the guys?" Juliet asked.

"I kicked them out of the kitchen and into the den. Anthony's been shopping." I pointed to the massive bag of baby items on the chair.

Wade held his hands up in surrender. "I heard the word baby, so I'm out like trout." He grabbed a beer out of the refrigerator and scurried out of the kitchen.

Juliet narrowed her eyes. "What does that even mean? Out like trout? I mean, fish flop around and die if we take them out of the water. Men make no sense sometimes."

I drizzled olive oil into a pan and added my chopped veggies. "I'm sure they say the same thing about you and I and our weird expressions."

"Did Anthony talk to Lu?"

"No. He says he has a plan and asked us not to say anything to her."

"I don't have a problem with it. Lu carries a gun and a big stick. Her hormones are in full mama bear mode right now. Girl Scout rule one says to avoid a mother bear protecting her cub." Juliet poured herself a glass of wine.

"You were a fantastic Girl Scout."

"I was, wasn't I? Girl Scouts taught me I had the potential to be anything I wanted. I could be an astronaut right now if I wanted to."

"No, you couldn't. Besides, it would be a weird career move."

Juliet considered my words, then shrugged. "Regardless, I'm staying away from the whole Lu and Anthony debacle."

"Good choice." I added Italian sausage to the

pan. "I talked to Mom about the guy in the photo. His name is Dean Winters."

"Did you find out any dirt?" Juliet asked.

"It's Mom. One does not find dirt on one's own mother." I waved the wooden spatula at her. "She dated him, but he disappeared the summer before she left for college. She said she never saw him after the night of the Founder's Day celebration in 1979."

"Curious. Was he murdered that night?" Juliet dug around in my utensil drawer and pulled out a bottle opener. "Did you tell her your theory that the guy in the grave might be her Dean Winters?"

"Yes, and he's not her Dean Winters. They had a brief fling, but she argued that night with him. It also means Mom is a suspect for his murder." I stabbed at the ground sausage in the pan as I tried to imagine my mother in prison orange. It would wreak havoc with her complexion.

"It's Mom. She wouldn't hurt a flea. I've seen her carry spiders out into the garden rather than hurt them. We have nothing to worry about, even if it turns out to be him in your yard."

I hoped Juliet was right, but I also knew from mystery novels how often the cops got it wrong. With my newfound promise to focus solely on the library and leave the criminals to Clint, I hoped everyone saw my mom like I did-a law-abiding citizen who never even had a parking ticket.

Two hours later, we sat at the kitchen table groaning from the copious amount of food and wine we had consumed. Anthony no longer looked as haunted as he had the previous evening, and Wade and Juliet were chatting about honeymoon locations.

"You could always have a destination wedding," I suggested.

"No way," Juliet said. "If we're going to do this whole establishment thing, we're going to do it one hundred percent right. It's important that all of our friends and family are present."

"Yeah," I agreed. "Mom would kill you if you didn't have Great Aunt June and all the horrible cousins at the ceremony."

"Cousin Ronald." Juliet wrinkled her nose in disgust. "Maybe we should elope, Wade."

"Fine by me," Wade said. "We could use all the money were saving for a down payment on a house."

The thought of my sister with a mortgage made me grin. It was so establishment. I knew she would come over to the nerd side. Who knew it would take someone like Wade, with his rough good looks and military ways, to convert Juliet?

"I don't want to talk about wedding plans anymore," Juliet said. "I'm not deciding anything until the curse on Phee disappears, and we solve the case of the body in the backyard."

"That's such a Nancy Drew title," I said. "I'm off crime solving. Plus, I have too much to take care of at the library, and honestly, it's a job for the professionals. I'm confident that Lu will figure out who shot our skeleton. It will be the same person who killed Mr. Muldean."

Juliet gave me an incredulous look. She put her

hand on my forehead and grabbed my wrist to take my pulse. "Holy guacamole, Clint! She's dying!" Juliet exclaimed.

I yanked my hand away. "I'm not dying. Our new board member said my immersion in crime is unseemly. I love the library and don't want to lose my job, so from now on, I'm sticking to the books. Scout's honor."

"You were never a Girl Scout," Clint said. "Juliet was."

"Brownie. Girl Scout. Close enough," I said. "Either way, I'm out of it. Just tell Lu she needs to solve this case. I've got a wedding to help plan."

Chapter Eleven

To be fair, I meant what I had said. I planned to keep my nose to myself. I was done with crime unless it was between the pages of a mystery novel. My promise went straight past the pew and out the door when I went to church on Sunday with my parents.

Clint had been called into work since the deputy normally scheduled had called out from food poisoning. Anyone who eats sushi from a gas station in Burlington, or any gas station regardless of location, deserves to be sick. I was worshiping solo this morning. I had invited Anthony, but he begged off, citing an appointment to help launch "Plan B for Baby." He had called the senator and extended his time off. I hoped he wouldn't be devastated if Lu refused to talk to him.

I slid into the pew next to my parents a few moments before the service started. My dad handed me a church bulletin. I saw they were asking for donations for the annual church rummage sale. I made a mental note to go through my closets to find a few items.

I glanced around at the congregation. Could any of these people be a murderer? I crossed off anyone under the age of sixty on the assumption that the same person who had murdered Craig had also murdered Dean. Could the murderer be Ralph Northstrum, who had been the school janitor for thirty-plus years? Or perhaps it was Alice Coleman, the former town clerk?

Fortunately, the choir began singing at that moment, and Reverend Taylor took the pulpit disrupting my musings before I convinced myself that

Patty Martin, a ninety-year-old piano teacher, had bludgeoned Craig with her metronome. Turning my attention to the sermon, I tried to absorb the morning's message rather than convict half the town of a crime they didn't commit.

After the service, I lingered. I told my parents I would see them at the house. I wanted to talk to Reverend Taylor about Graham Lawson. Unfortunately, several of the ladies surrounded him wanting to discuss summer vacation bible school.

"How are you, Phee?" Mrs. Taylor came up to me, a big smile on her face. An older woman, she was the perfect complement to Reverend Taylor. He was a charismatic leader who gave rousing sermons. She was a quiet woman with a calm manner that soothed crying babies and held the hands of the ill in their hospital bed.

"I'm good. Things are gearing up for VBS. I should be able to come help at least one day. It's on my calendar."

"Excellent. We always appreciate any volunteers."

"May I ask you what you know about Graham Lawson, Mrs. Taylor?"

"I hear he's a fine preacher," Mrs. Taylor said, sidestepping the question.

"He's a new member of the library's board of trustees. I'm afraid I didn't make a good impression on him."

Reverend and Mrs. Taylor were not gossips. I could not say the same of some members of the congregation. She hesitated, then said, "I believe that a

65

church is made strong by its people, not by the dollars in its coffers. Graham Lawson delivers a fine sermon and knows his scripture, but I like our small church. I don't feel we need a big building to accomplish our mission."

"Have we lost members to the new church?" I asked.

"A few. Some folks always like the next new shiny thing. They are all about the best and brightest." She patted my shoulder. "It's not for me to judge them. I can only pray they find what they need. The only thing I can tell you is Reverend Lawson likes those in his inner circle to appear above reproach."

I nodded my understanding. "He disapproves of my penchant for stumbling on murders."

"You have had a string of misfortune in that area, haven't you? It will be fine. You are an asset to this community, and we're fortunate you've chosen to stay in Miller's Cove."

I thanked her and decided that any conversation with Reverend Taylor would have to take place another day. My mother served Sunday dinner promptly at one o'clock. My brother, Rick, and his family were planning on coming, and I was excited to see the twins.

When I got to Mom and Dad's, Rick and Carrie's minivan was already parked in the driveway. I maneuvered Velma behind Dad's old Volvo and headed inside with ten minutes to spare before Mom's one o'clock Sunday dinner deadline. Juliet had texted me to let me know that Wade's prosthetic leg had rubbed a spot raw, so he was in the wheelchair for the day to give it a chance to heal. She planned to stay home in case he needed anything. I figured she wanted to avoid my interrogation of Mom.

In the kitchen, my mother gave a pointed look at the clock on the wall. She was busy putting dinner on serving plates. Sunday was the one day of the week when my parents tried to instill a bit of civility into family dinners with good china and vegetables in serving dishes rather than dished up straight from the saucepans. I took the bowls and placed them in the center of the table, then went to find the rest of the family.

I tracked them down in Dad's man cave. Carrie and Rick were on the floor playing with the twins, and my dad was lazily scratching our Irish Setter, Hamlet.

"My gosh, you two better come give Auntie Phee a kiss!" I grabbed Zoe, who squealed loudly and tried to wriggle out of arms.

Samuel was quietly banging on a toy car with his mini construction hammer. He endured my hugs and kisses without pausing in his determined destruction.

"Hey, Flea. Is Clint with you?" Rick stood up and gave me a half hug.

"Good to see you, too. I'm fine. Thanks for asking," I said.

Since Rick and Clint had been friends since they were kids, I didn't take really take offense, but I couldn't resist the opportunity to give my big brother grief. He rolled his eyes, ignoring the jibe.

"I only dress him. I've had no success trying to civilize your brother. Your parents are to blame."

Carrie said, a laugh taking the bite from her words. She wiped Zoe's runny nose.

"It's their mother's fault," Dad said. "She's quite mad."

"Well, she'll definitely lose it if we don't go sit down for dinner. And to answer your question, Clint had to work," I said. I picked Samuel up and took the hammer out of his hand. "You can play with Auntie Phee after dinner, Sammy."

Samuel stared at me and grunted. Unlike his sister, Zoe, who chattered nonstop, Samuel rarely spoke. Carrie said he was practicing becoming the strong, silent type when he grew up.

Dinner was a noisy affair, with Rick sharing updates from his work as an architect and Carrie telling funny stories about some of her students at the local elementary school. I loved Sunday dinners with my family. It was a tradition I hoped I could pass on one day to my own children. Our numbers varied from week to week depending on what we had going on in our own lives, but usually at least one sibling and their significant other sat at the table by one o'clock each week.

"So, any news on your investigation?" Rick asked when we had all finished eating.

"I am hands off since I have no interest in dead bodies or murders," I said. I didn't even have to lie. As far as I was concerned, my involvement was done.

"I guess I won't need to show you some pictures of Dean I found in the attic," Mom said.

Curiosity made my ears perk up. "Pictures?

Well, it wouldn't hurt for me to get to know the guy who's been sharing space in my yard."

"Wait? Who is Dean? Mom, you knew the victim?" Rick asked.

I explained to him we hadn't received confirmation of the man's identity, but based on a few clues, I surmised he was Dean Winters, a member of a local band in the seventies and Mom's former boyfriend.

"You dated him?" Rick asked my mother. He looked bewildered that my mother had dated someone other than our father. I knew I wasn't the only one who had difficulty imagining their parents and teachers in any other light but their proscribed roles.

"Your mother was and still is quite a looker," my dad said. He peered sadly at the small bowl of strawberry gelatin in front of him, then looked longingly at the key lime pie on my plate. My mother still had him on a strict diet. I knew he had a secret stash, but he had sworn me to secrecy.

"I would still like to see them," I said, "for purely intellectual reasons, not investigative."

"Of course," Mom said, giving me a fishy-eyed stare of disbelief.

I helped Mom clean up while everyone else went to the backyard to let the twins play on their new swing set my parents recently built. I washed while she dried and put things away in the cupboards.

"Do you think it is him?" Mom asked.

I knew in my gut that it was him, and I felt she needed to know what it could mean for her. "Yeah,

Mom, I do. I think he disappeared the same night you last saw him." I drained the water from the sink and dried my hands on a dish towel.

Mom was quiet while she put the last few dishes up, then motioned for me to follow her. We went into Rick's old room, which was now the guest bedroom. She opened the closet and took an old photo album off the shelf.

"Come look," Mom said. She sat on the bed and opened the album, flipping through the pages until she found what she was looking for.

I sat down next to her, and she handed me the album. There were four photographs on the page. Slightly faded from age, the faces were still clearly identifiable. The pictures depicted the same faces in each–four men and two girls. My mom was easily recognizable with her long, blonde hair. In each of the snapshots, Dean Winters had his arm slung around her shoulders, and she was staring at him with a look I recognized as love. I knew that look because it was the same way I stared at Clint when I was a teenager. Honestly, I looked at him the same way now.

I peered closely. The faces looked familiar. "Who are all these other people?"

"You should know all of them. Well, except for this guy, Graham Lawson. He left that summer, too." She pointed to the guy with long, dark brown hair that touched his shoulders and a cheesy mustache.

I snapped my fingers. That's why he looked so familiar to me that day at the library. He was one of the guys in the band and in the newspaper photograph.

"I've had the misfortune of meeting him. He's my newest board member. He also has the new church on the outskirts of town."

"I'm surprised to hear that," Mom said.

"What? That he moved back to town?"

"Well, that, too, but Graham Lawson had such a loose concept of right and wrong when were young that I'm surprised he chose the church." Mom shrugged her shoulders. "People change. Hopefully, he's learned to control his temper. He was such a hothead. I remember he got angry when Dean screwed up a song. Graham threw a bottle of beer at him. Dean had to get eight stitches. After that, I stayed away from rehearsals."

My mother's words moved Graham Lawson from the jerk category to suspect. I looked at some of the other faces and recognized the blonde man from the newspaper clipping. I pointed to him. "That's Craig Muldean,"

"It sure is. He was always on the fringes of the band. He was part of it, but not, if that makes sense."

"I'm not sure what you mean."

"He played drums," Mom said. "He was good, but he lacked the drive and passion for music. Dean lived, breathed, talked about music twenty-four seven. He was determined to make it big, which is why I assumed he had left to go to California."

She shook her head. "But for Craig, music seemed like something he used to fit in. Craig had such a crush on Sheila. It was actually sort of sad the way he mooned around after her."

"Sheila?" I asked.

71

"Sheila Dawes. Well, back then, she was Sheila Croft." Mom pointed to the other girl.

I should have recognized her. Sheriff Dawes and his wife, Sheila, had been friends with my parents since before I was born. "I take it Sheila didn't return Craig's interest."

Mom laughed. "Not at all. She was crazy about some guy, but she would never tell me who it was, even though she was my best friend back then."

"You and Sheila are still friends," I said, surprised to hear my mom and Sheila had been so close. Although my dad and the sheriff were close, I had always assumed my mother had become friends with Sheila because of the men.

"Things changed that summer. Not all of it was good. I could never quite figure it out, but after the Founder's Day celebration, we all drifted apart. It happened rather quickly now that I think back on it."

"Who was this guy?" I pointed to the last person. Although I couldn't bring his name to mind, he looked familiar, too.

"Sam LeVere. So sad."

I didn't need her to say anything else. Sam LeVere had died in a horrible farm accident outside of town ten years ago. I had been at college, but I heard about it from Juliet when I had come home for the summer. He caught his arm in a threshing machine and died before anyone could save him.

"We had so much fun that summer. I was sad when Dean left, but I didn't blame him for wanting more. Miller's Cove constrained him, and he needed something bigger and brighter than what he could find here." Her finger traced her friends' faces. "It's funny. Graham, Craig, Sam, Sheila, Monty, and me. If we left Miller's Cove, we still all came back. Well, except for Craig. He stayed put. He did pretty well for himself."

"Monty?" I asked. I had only counted six people in the picture.

Mom took the album from me and closed it. She put it back on the closet shelf. "Monty James, the mayor. He was the one behind the camera–always watching and recording our lives. He was the band's 'promoter.'" Mom used air quotes and grimaced.

"It's a good thing Mr. James went into politics, since it seems like you thought so little of his promoting skills," I said.

"Are you done with your interrogation?" Mom asked.

"Interrogation? I wasn't interrogating you."

Mom laughed. "You can tell us you won't investigate Dean's murder and you might even believe it yourself, but I know you. You can't walk away from a mystery."

She was right. There was a need to know the answer that was almost addictive. I had to see this through, but I would have to be discreet and stay under the library board's radar.

When I arrived home that evening, Clint was still at the station. I fed Ferdie, the world's fattest cat with an attitude, and took the dogs for a walk. By the time we returned home, Clint's truck was in the driveway, backed up to our chain link fence.

AMY E. LILLY

I found him in the bedroom, changing out of his uniform and into the hideous t-shirt he always wore to work on his truck or do yard work. I swore he kept it around just to make me crazy. It had several holes that grew with every wash, and it had gone from a white with a collar of green and some sort of old beer logo to dingy gray with a questionable few letters remaining.

"My parents send their love, and my mother sent a plate for you. Would you like for me to heat it up?" I kissed him.

"Maybe later. They officially released the backyard as a crime scene, so I'm going to refill the hole where the shed was. I brought a load of fill dirt from the construction site of the new church."

"You mean the uber church, home of the oh-so-proper Graham Lawson?" I grabbed a pair of jeans and a t-shirt from my dresser to change out of my church clothes so I could help. "How come they've released the scene?"

"Sheriff Dawes said they've got all they can from the scene. They've identified the body, too. You were right. It was Dean Winters."

I sat down on the bed. Before, he was just a skeleton and a guy in a photograph. It wasn't a known fact. Now, I knew that this was a person with actual dreams and talent. Heck, he must have been a decent guy if my mom had dated him.

"I have something to tell you," I said. I slipped on some tennis shoes and avoided Clint's eyes by slowly tying the laces. "My mom was possibly the last person to see Dean Winters alive the night he disappeared."

"What?" Clint's voice rose. "Why didn't you tell me this the other day? Damn it, Phee. I could get in big trouble with the sheriff if he thinks I'm hiding evidence because of a family connection."

"I didn't tell you because there hadn't been an identification. It could have been someone else. Why drag my mom into something that might have nothing to do with her at all?" My voice rose in volume to match his.

Clint pulled his cell phone out of his pocket. "I've got to make a phone call."

I wanted to stop him, but the look he gave me said it wasn't something he could ignore. A moment later, I heard him talking to Lu. I didn't want to eavesdrop, but since it involved family, I had no choice.

"Could you wait until tomorrow, Lu? Thanks. I appreciate it."

I scurried back from the doorway and bent down to straighten a nonexistent cuff problem.

"Lu said she would go talk to your mom tomorrow. She'll have to make an official statement. There's no way we can keep her out of this investigation."

"I understand," I said. And I did. He and Lu had a job to do. "Are you angry with me?"

"No." He pulled me into his arms. "You're right. Until we knew for sure who it was, it wasn't relevant. Plus, it's not like your mom's going to go on the lam."

"I don't know. She and Juliet could pull a

75

Thelma and Louise and run off to the Grand Canyon," I said.

"You and Juliet, yes. Your mom? That woman doesn't have a law-breaking bone in her body."

Clint would soon regret those words. Turns out everyone has a past–even my mom.

Chapter Twelve

"I can't believe you did a Pepper Anderson on Mom," Juliet said. She sprinkled the top of her soy latte with some cinnamon and took a sip. "Perfect. Once again, Nellie, you made me the perfect drink."

"I've been practicing some of those la di da drinks they have at the chain coffee places in Burlington," Nellie said with a satisfied grin. "My soy latte is pretty dang good and won't empty your wallet. My scones are better, too. Not that I'm bragging or anything."

Since my mouth was full of one of her blueberry lemon scones, I had to agree. I was working at the library from noon to closing today, and Juliet had a quick break before her next yoga class. I called her this morning to let her know all the news. Nellie Jo, never one to miss a chance to pass the time chatting, had joined us at our table when the morning rush had cleared.

"Pepper Anderson was a little tougher on criminals in *Police Woman* than I was on Mom," I said. "Mom volunteered the information. Sheila Dawes was friends with Dean Winters, too."

"Dang. I wouldn't want to be the one who tried to nose around in the sheriff's business," Nellie said. "I try to stay on the good side of the law after all of Mike and his kin's shenanigans."

Someone had killed Nellie's husband, Mike, and stuffed him in a pickle vat at his factory. The sheriff had suspected Nellie Jo of the murder until Juliet and I discovered the criminal. We had almost gone to the enormous library in the sky when the culprit's pet alligator, Ethel, came close to eating us for a snack. I'd sworn off getting a pet lizard ever since that night.

"Mom's the last person to see Dean alive." I lowered my voice. "She's a suspect. Any investigator knows you can't allow personal feelings to cloud the investigation."

"Mom's not a suspect!" Juliet exclaimed, then lowered her voice. "The killer was the last person to see Dean, not our mother. The woman served as president of our PTA when we were growing up for goddess's sake. She's a tenured professor. People like her don't kill people and jaunt back to college."

"The guy that committed a bunch of bombings went to Harvard. Education doesn't eliminate a criminal mind," I said. "We have to consider Mom a suspect until we can eliminate her."

Juliet appeared skeptical but said nothing else as I laid out my plan of investigation. "I'm going to dig around in the newspaper archives this afternoon in between patrons. I want to see who else had close ties to this band. Nellie Jo, can you ask around to see if anyone was acting suspicious after they found the skeleton?"

"Well, I'm not one to gossip, but I suppose it can't hurt to listen in on other people's conversations. Lots of folks don't mind their p's and q's when they're shooting the breeze in here, so I overhear lots of stuff that I don't pass on. Why just the other day, I found out that Lana Oglethorpe got liposuction, but she told everyone that she had her gallbladder removed."

I interrupted before Nellie told us any more gossip she had accidentally overheard. "Juliet, can you talk to Sheila? I don't know how you'll bring up Dean without it being awkward, but I have faith you'll come up with something."

Juliet grabbed a piece of my scone from my plate and popped it in her mouth. "She's signed up to take my beginning Reiki class, so I'm on it. I'll be the Cagney to your Lacey, the Starsky to your Hutch– "

"Got it. No need to elaborate, oh so dramatic one. Could you please update your viewer preferences? A cop show from the nineties would add a little spice to your repertoire," I said. My sister and her obsession with cheesy seventies cop shows was peppering her personality with bad one-liners from the shows. "Also, Juls, I need you to clear your calendar for Wednesday night. Nellie, you're welcome to come along. Willow already is on board."

"Where are we going?" Juliet asked.

"To the Wednesday night service by suspect number three, Graham Lawson."

At noon, I entered the library to find Wade engrossed in conversation with Reverend Taylor. Wade, while not a religious man, did like to engage in deep theological discussions. An ex-Marine badly injured in the war, Wade had spent much of his recovery time reading an eclectic mix of nonfiction and fiction. It had helped distract him from the pain he was enduring. Now, he used that knowledge to engage in intelligent debates when the occasion arose.

"I see you found another worthy opponent besides my father for your theological debates, Reverend," I said. I glanced down at the book in his hand. Reverend Taylor certainly enjoyed some dark thrillers and police procedurals. He had told me they helped keep him awake during his long vigils next to hospital beds for members of our congregation.

"I have the latest mystery by the author your wife likes," I said. "Would you like it?"

Mrs. Taylor favored cozy mysteries. She chose books with recipes or crafts included. I didn't mind. I often benefited from her testing out the recipes she found in the back of her favorite author's novels. Wade said goodbye to the reverend and went to help Mr. Collins find a western he hadn't read.

I grabbed the novel for Mrs. Taylor and returned to the circulation desk. "I meant to speak to you on Sunday, Reverend. Graham Lawson is our newest library board member. I hadn't had the chance to get to know him prior to our first meeting. Have you had much of an opportunity to chat with him?" I asked. I scanned the barcode on the back of the book, then handed it to him.

The reverend spoke slowly, measuring his words. "I had the chance to speak with him briefly. Although we are not so far apart in our interpretation of the good book, we part ways over fiscal matters."

"I heard he requires people to tithe automatically from their bank accounts. I guess he needs to ensure they finish building the enormous church."

"I've heard rumors, but I put little stock in gossip. I believe he's from Miller's Cove originally."

"Did you know him?" I asked.

Reverend Taylor shook his head. "Before my time, I'm afraid. The wife and I came here in the early eighties. Well, I best be going. I promised Mrs. Harris I would stop by and say a prayer for her Schnauzer. He's been having breathing problems."

"I hope she's taken him to the vet. Not that prayer would hurt," I hurried to add.

"She has. She told me she wants to make extra sure, just in case. Have a good day, Phee, and tell that sister of yours to not be a stranger."

He waved goodbye, taking his books with him. Reverend Taylor hadn't told me anything I didn't already know about Graham. I guess it was a good thing I'd already put Operation Uberchurch Recon together for Wednesday night.

Wade left for lunch. Mondays were slow, and our library clerk didn't come in until after the high school released. I spent the next hour reading book reviews and choosing books for the next month's order. Although we were in a small, rural library, a healthy property tax levy that included the lake cottages guaranteed I had a decent budget to spend on books and programming. Unfortunately, the monies didn't extend to additional help except in the summer. I couldn't complain. During the winter months, the population dwindled to year-round residents, so I supplemented staff with high school students after school and during the summer to help shelve and run programs for the

81

youngest patrons.

When Wade returned from lunch, I went to the microfilm and pulled out the year prior to Dean's disappearance. I wanted to see if I could find more information about his band and bandmates. I delved into the dizzying reels of microfilm. It was one of my least favorite tasks as a librarian. I never understood how some of my more avid genealogists could sit for hours on end searching for obituaries as they reconstructed their family tree.

I looked at the time prior to Dean's death and found the occasional mention of several of the band's members, as well as my mom and Sheila. Unfortunately, all references were for academic achievements or athletic awards. No smoking guns with anyone that I found. It was interesting to see what was happening in Miller's Cove back before it became such a hot summer vacation spot with the expansion of the lake cottages.

I slowed the reel to skim some more articles. There wasn't too much happening in the sleepy town. An occasional article about grand openings and an article about crop circles appearing in local farmers' fields. There had even been a bank robbery at the First National Bank that spring. Three masked men had entered the bank right before closing and had left with an undisclosed amount of cash. Louis Partridge had been sheriff, and the front page had featured an oversized photograph of him outside of the bank.

I skimmed through several more articles, but I couldn't find mention of the police solving the bank robbery. If they had had a woman like Lu on the force back then, the robbers would have been too terrified of the deputies to risk robbing the bank. I slowed the reel. There was a small article on page two about another bank robbery in nearby Crofton. Three masked men had been the perpetrators in the robbery.

I chuckled. My parents always said they stayed in Miller's Cove because it was a safe, crime-free area, but it looked to be the hotbed of criminal activity in the seventies. Since I hadn't found additional information about the band members, I couldn't waste more time. I still had to finish working on programming ideas for summer reading. It might be two months away, but I wanted to make sure I had volunteers to help with the children and enough supplies. Investigating would have to wait for another time.

Chapter Thirteen

For the next two days, I stayed busy with library business. I talked at the local Ladies Auxiliary monthly luncheon on Tuesday. I promoted upcoming programs and explained all the ways we could help seniors with computer classes, book clubs and personalized help with family history. By the end of the day, I had grown two feet in confidence alone. Graham wouldn't be able to claim I neglected my duties as the public face of the library. I was a darn good librarian, despite what some people might say.

The next morning, I opened the library. I hosted a toddler story time and Willow had promised to come help. Our theme was yoga tales. As I read the story, Willow would guide the students through yoga poses resembling the animals in the story. Usually Juliet helped, but she had a class in Burlington to take. She wanted to expand her class offerings at her studio, so she was doing something related to hot yoga. Personally, the thought of doing yoga in a hot room surrounded by people with swamp butt was unappealing.

At a quarter to ten, Willow breezed into the library, followed by a teenage girl with dark hair and wearing the same flowing style of clothing.

"Phee, sorry I'm late. This is my cousin, Izzy. Her parents sent her to visit me over her spring break," Willow said.

"Nice to meet you, Izzy. You're welcome to help with the class if you'd like," I said. Wrangling wiggly toddlers was always a challenge, so additional hands were always welcome.

"Um, I'd rather read if it's okay with you. Crumb snatchers aren't really my thing," Izzy said, wrinkling her nose. "Little kids kind of freak me out."

I laughed. They sometimes freaked me out, too. Of course, I was more concerned with the idea that I might one day have a little crumb snatcher of my own to take care of and love. "Sure. Our YA section is over there."

"Thanks." Izzy wandered over to the comfortable chairs arranged by the shelves dedicated to our teen readers. She grabbed one of the new releases and plopped down in a seat. Putting her ear buds in, she had effectively tuned Willow, the toddlers, and me out for the duration.

"What's going on with the dead guy?" Willow asked. She pulled a yoga mat from her bag and rolled it out over the carpet.

"His name is Dean Winters. My mom dated him right before he disappeared," I said. "He was in the band called the Screaming Goats. It was him, Craig Muldean, Graham Lawson, and Sam LeVere."

"Two people out of a band of four guys are dead. Sounds like someone might have a grudge against them. I have a grudge against them because of their name. Why are the goats screaming? Animal cruelty is an actual issue in the country right now."

I didn't disagree with Willow about the problem of animal cruelty. However, I'm sure the band had nothing to do with anything related to goats. To me, it sounded like a random name thought up after a few too many beers.

"You're right about animal cruelty," I said. "I'm going to Graham Lawson's church tonight with Juliet. I'm hoping to find out a little more about who he was back then. He left town not too long after Dean disappeared. Highly suspicious."

"Please let me go with you." Willow put her hands together in a pleading gesture. "I am all about trying to connect with God, the goddesses, and the surrounding spirits, but I've heard too many rumors about this church to not go, too."

I hesitated for only a second. Willow was always laid back and open to everyone's belief system. Even if this evening turned out to be an infomercial for religion, she would be the voice of reason when Juliet and I might not be. "Okay. Meet me at the house at five thirty. We need a definite plan. The three of us can divide and conquer the congregation to see what people might know."

"Four," Izzy chimed in from her chair. "I'm in."

"Four, it is," I said.

Willow and I didn't talk more about the case because the toddlers streamed into the library with their tired moms trailing behind them. For the next thirty minutes, I growled like a bear and roared like a lion while Willow guided the three-year-olds through a series of poses. Even two mothers joined in, although the majority sat nearby taking a much-deserved break from their day.

I arrived home a few minutes after five and

hurried to change out of my stretchy pants and flowing long top. On toddler days, I tried to wear comfortable clothing that allowed me to get up and down off the floor with ease. I changed into a flowered blouse with a ruffled collar and a knee-length blue skirt. Even though I despised them, I encased myself into a pair of pantyhose and low-heeled blue pumps. Something told me this was the proper attire to wear to the Uber Church. I always wore a dress to Miller's Cove Community Church, but I felt comfortable enough to go without hose. I doubted Graham approved of naked-legged ladies.

When Juliet arrived with Willow and Izzy pulling in behind her, I was relieved to see they had donned more conservative clothing as well.

"How do you like my disguise?" Juliet did a quick pirouette. She had pulled her long blond hair into a tight bun, and she wore a denim skirt with a plain white blouse.

"You look like a housewife from the eighties," I said.

"I blend."

"Personally, I wanted to wear normal clothes," Willow said, "but this one said you can't go undercover as yourself."

Izzy shrugged her shoulders. "I watch a lot of cop shows. You can't stand out when trailing a suspect."

Juliet clutched her hands to her chest. "A girl after my heart."

Willow wore a long-sleeved loose t-shirt that

was logo free with a patchwork skirt and clogs. Izzy had chosen a button-down men's style shirt with a plain A-line skirt and flats. She hadn't worn hose. I envied her.

"Where's Clint?" Juliet asked as we walked into my living room.

"He's with Lu following up on questioning some of Craig's neighbors. One of them wasn't home when they went door to door the day of the murder, so he thought they would have better luck in the evening."

"Makes sense," Willow said, nodding.

"Anthony is off doing mysterious things that he refuses to tell me, but he said if we run into trouble, he's only a cell phone call away," I said.

"What's the plan?" Juliet asked.

I sat down on my over-sized chaise lounge chair. "We're going to get there early and mingle. Ask them about the church. See if anyone remembers Graham when he lived here before. I need to get a better picture of this guy. After the service, I'll chat with his wife and see what she knows about why he left Miller's Cove."

"Sounds good," Willow said. "I may have to plant a few seeds of disharmony among the worshipers. This place smacks of corporate greed and the establishment."

She and Juliet bumped fists like a duo of teenage boys. I rolled my eyes. Besides their love of all things New Age, Willow and Juliet protested anything related to big corporations and the male patriarchy. It always amazed me that Juliet and Wade, with his former military service, worked so well together.

"Whatever you do, don't make a scene. This guy is still on my library board. Be subtle," I said.

Izzy laughed. "Subtle is not a word in Willow's vocabulary. This is going to be spectacular. I wish I had brought popcorn so I could sit back and enjoy the chaos."

Unfortunately, my gut told me Izzy was right. It was a good thing the rest of the library board liked me.

We arrived twenty minutes prior to the start of the church service. Enough time to mingle without being awkward. It surprised me to see several members of my church in the seats. I spotted Gladys Dorset near the front and peeled myself away from the others to chat with her.

"Ophelia Jefferson, it is so good to see you. How's your mama and daddy?" Gladys grasped my hand and pulled me down in the seat next to her.

Gladys was arguably the biggest gossip in town. Between her and Cincinnati, the two of them covered the circuit of coffee klatches, craft groups, men's clubs, and everything in between.

"They're both doing well," I said. "I didn't know you stopped attending our church."

Gladys waved my comment away. "Oh, I haven't. I just like to come to this service on Wednesday because it's closer to my house. I can make it home in time for my shows and not even miss the opening credits."

"I understand."

She lowered her voice and said, "I'm not joining

this congregation because I'm on a fixed income. I watch my pennies. Mrs. Taylor brings me casseroles and baked goods. On my budget, it's always nice to have a little help."

I leaned in. "Is it true you have to give Graham Lawson access to your bank account?"

Gladys glanced around her before answering. "You do. Poor Connie ended up bouncing a check at the Shop-N-Save after they pulled money from her account at the beginning of the month before her Social Security went in. It mortified her, and now she has to go shop for groceries in Burlington."

I chatted with Gladys a few more minutes about her rheumatism and her son, Charlie, who had moved "three states away and was dating a nice girl from Omaha." I pried myself away with a promise that I would have my mother stop by and visit.

I spotted Juliet talking to Mr. Roper at the back of the room. I wandered over and joined them.

"He was a wild one," Mr. Roper said. "If he hadn't joined the military, I'm sure he would have done time. He's turned himself around and made something of himself."

"Really? What kind of trouble did Graham get into?" Juliet asked, wide-eyed and innocent. She should have been on stage.

Mr. Roper chuckled. "Nothing too awful. A bit of shoplifting and he and his group of friends would hold loud parties out in the woods near the lake. Bunch of drinking and smoking dope, but it was enough to cause his parents some grief."

"He clearly had an epiphany. Graham's got quite a following here," Juliet said, sweeping her arm around to the growing congregation.

"He's a good preacher." Mr. Roper nodded. He turned to me and held out his hand. "How are you, Phee? I've been meaning to stop by the library, but I've been so busy being retired I haven't had a chance."

"Come by anytime. I'd love to see you. Were you talking about Reverend Lawson? I heard he used to be friends with Craig Muldean and Dean Winters. He must be quite upset with the news that they both died."

Mr. Roper's lips tightened. "Craig Muldean was alright, and he did the right thing taking over the hardware store when his father died all those years ago, but Dean Winters…"

"Dean what?" I prodded.

Mr. Roper shook his head. "I won't speak ill of the dead, especially not in church. Talk to your mama if you want to know about Dean. For a time, everyone thought the two of them might get married."

Before I had time to process that bit of news, the music signaling the start of the service played. Juliet and I scurried to find a seat. Willow and Izzy slid in next to us.

"While you two have been chitchatting, Izzy and I found something interesting," Willow whispered.

"What?" Juliet asked.

The woman sitting in front of us turned her head to shush us. Chastened, I gave Willow a questioning look. Willow lowered her voice even more. Juliet and I leaned in as close as we could. "Reverend Lawson's in deep with some shady corporations. If love of money is the root of all evil, then Graham Lawson might just be the devil himself."

"Shhh!"

"Sorry," I said, lowering my head. Not wanting to risk the pew shusher, I focused on the service.

Graham's style was more bombastic than Reverend Taylor, but I couldn't fault his message. He emphasized kindness and compassion for sinners, and to hate the sin, not the person. Easy to say, but it was sometimes difficult to practice.

Unlike our services, they did not pass the collection plate around the congregation at the end. Instead, Graham encouraged support through monthly donations and ushers handed out forms to those who raised their hands. Out of curiosity, I took one.

How convenient. The form had a place to staple your voided check, or you could tithe via your credit card. To me, it smacked of paying a bill rather than something you did because of devotion. Willow took it out of my hands. She crumpled it, and to my shock, she threw it on the floor. With her eco-friendly ways, littering was a mortal sin.

We filed out the door. Several people stopped to speak with Graham, and a few of the older ladies chatted a little longer than was polite.

"Miss Jefferson, I'm surprised to see you here."

Before I could respond, Willow stepped in front of me. "What do you do with all the money you fleece these people out of?" Willow's face was red, and her voice shook. "Selling faith, Reverend?"

Graham took a step back. "I don't sell religion, and I certainly don't fleece people. Who are you? Miss Jefferson, is this *woman* a friend of yours?" His lip curled.

"Um…" I didn't know how to respond. I'd never seen Willow angry. Impassioned over a wrong, yes, but angry and confrontational was something I never thought I would see.

"Did you come here just to disrupt my service, you, and your friends?" He wrinkled his nose as if he smelled something rotten. "I can see I was right to be concerned about you being the face of an esteemed institute like the Miller's Cove Public Library. You lack the decorum and respectability the position requires. The company you keep is a clear sign that you're not suited to be a community leader."

"Listen, you pompous snake oil charlatan!" Willow shook her finger in Graham's face.

Izzy grabbed her arm and pulled her back. "Let's go, Willow."

Shaken, I pushed past some people who had lingered in the doorway during Willow's outburst. Juliet quickly caught up. I leaned against Velma and took a calming breath.

"Phee, slow down."

"I expected you to lose your cool, but Willow? What the heck was she thinking? I could lose my job!"

Willow and Izzy joined us. "Sorry," Willow said. "I lost it. I can't stand people who take money from the elderly and the poor. They're the ones most likely to give their life savings away to a con man like

93

that because they need hope."

"I get it, but making a scene will not help," I said. "Let's just go home. Maybe all of this will blow over."

We rode in silence. When we arrived at my house, I said goodnight and trudged inside. Clint still wasn't home, so I made myself a cup of peppermint tea and took the dogs into the backyard.

Watson and Fritz darted to the fence and sniffed around in a tizzy. They could smell the neighbor's cat, Fuzz, who would occasionally stray into my yard. Ferdie would hiss and spit when he spotted Fuzz, but he kept to the safety of the porch rather than engage. Watson dug furiously at a spot near where the garden shed had stood. He shoved his nose into the dirt like a pig hunting for truffles.

"Watson, stop digging!" I said sharply. I set my cup of tea down and went to see what had him tearing up my yard. He had a penchant for digging up moles, but I thought I eradicated them all last year.

In the twilight, I saw a glint of metal near the edge of the makeshift grave. I reached down and scraped the rest of the dirt away, Watson panting happily next to me. It was a key chain with a small key attached.

I whistled for the boys to follow me, and I went inside to inspect Watson's discovery further. I rinsed them off in the sink and patted the key chain and key dry with a paper towel. The key chain was hard plastic in the shape of the number one. There were a few letters and an image remaining, but I couldn't make out what it said. The key was stamped with a number, but no words.

It was just an old key, but my senses were telling me it was important. Now, I just had to find out why.

Chapter Fourteen

I was in bed, half asleep, by the time Clint arrived home. He slid quietly under the covers, trying not to wake me.

"G 'night," I mumbled.

"Good night, sweetheart. Go back to sleep," he whispered.

I drifted off with his arm around me and my mind whirling around about keys and people in sheep costumes with hundreds of Grahams shearing them of their fleece.

***

Clint woke me the next morning with coffee poured in my favorite librarian-themed coffee mug with the perfect splash of creamer and sugar. I pushed myself up and took the much-needed caffeine. I had not slept well, and the fear that I would face an angry board today made my stomach twist.

"You're up early," I said, once a couple of sips penetrated my sleep-addled brain.

He buttoned his khaki deputy's shirt. "I've got to get back in. The sheriff's really breathing down our necks to find out who killed Craig Muldean. Elections are this year and he and the mayor run on their platform of keeping Miller's Cove a safe, small town."

"Any progress?" I asked.

"Not really. The neighbor was home when Craig's murder took place, and she saw someone knock on his door. Unfortunately, the person had a baseball cap on, and she didn't see a car. The only description she gave us was that the person was athletic in build."

Clint looked exhausted. Stubble grew on his chin, and dark circles had formed under his eyes, so I decided to not burden him with my uber church fiasco of the previous evening. "I'm sure you'll figure it out. I have faith in you and Lu's ability to track down the truth," I said, taking another sip of coffee.

He raised an eyebrow. "What aren't you telling me? It's not like you to not ferret out more information. You have an insatiable appetite for mystery."

"Mystery isn't all I have an insatiable appetite for." I gave him a lecherous grin.

He leaned down and gave me a kiss. "I'm going to hold you to that," he promised. "I've got to run, or Lu will leave me behind. She's meaner than a feral cat guarding her kittens."

I laughed at the image in my mind of Lu with a passel of kittens. "Good luck. Bring her chocolate. Lots of chocolate."

After he left, I sat on the bed snuggled into the covers while I finished enjoying my coffee. I couldn't dally too long since I needed to get to work and open the library. I would do a great job while I still had one.

When I got to work, Cincinnati was outside waiting for me. A regular patron, he made his way through the town each day to visit his favorite haunts. The library was always first on the tour because my newspaper was free, and he liked to help me pull the books from the book drop. A lonely retiree, he liked to feel useful. To be honest, I expected my board members to be standing on the front steps of the library and demand my resignation. Of course, I realized that most of them had known me my entire life and wouldn't oust me without a better reason than Willow's outburst. Graham's disapproval of me as librarian rattled me. I had let him niggle his way into my brain and he had planted a seed of doubt.

"Hey, Cincinnati. How's it going?" I asked him. I unlocked the library doors and ushered him inside.

"Can't complain," he said. "Did you see the game last night?"

Cincinnati's real name was Charlie, but because of his obsession with the Cincinnati Reds, he had rightfully earned his nickname. Despite knowing I didn't follow baseball or football, he would always ask me if I watched the game.

"Sorry, no." I said. "I went to that new church last night."

Cincinnati gave me an odd look. He harrumphed and grabbed his newspaper and settled down on the couch to read it.

"What?" I asked. Cincinnati had an opinion on everything, and it wasn't like him not to share it.

"I knew Graham when he was a smart-mouthed kid. When I got back from Vietnam, he wanted to flap his gums about how I was a traitor. I threatened to punch him, and he ran away like a scared rabbit." He straightened his paper. "If you want to talk a big game, you need to back it up with action. Graham Lawson is all hot air. For all his chest thumping at me when he was a teen, he ended up joining the military himself."

"Don't worry," I said. "I'm not joining his

church. I'm more than happy where I'm at. Graham's my new board member. I wanted to investigate the lay of the land, so to speak." I didn't dare tell Cincinnati I suspected Graham's relation to Dean's and Craig's murders. If I had, the gossip would make its way through his entire daily route.

He just harrumphed again and rattled his paper. He said nothing else, so I went and turned on all the computers to prepare for the day.

When the phone rang at nine thirty, it startled me from my revelry at the front desk. Cincinnati had left, and I was mindlessly checking books in from the drop. "Miller's Cove Public Library. This is Phee speaking. How may I help you today?" I used my best customer service voice.

"Phee, Mayor James here. I'd like you to stop by and chat with me today if you would."

"Certainly. May I ask what this is about?" I asked. The mayor rarely visited the library, and he never called.

"I'll wait until you get here," he said.

I looked at my watch. Wade would arrive at ten. "I can stop by at ten thirty. Does that work?"

"See you then."

I placed the phone back in the cradle. I tried to ignore the knot that was slowly twisting in my stomach. The mayor never took an interest in the library. I spoke to him and the town council once a year to request the town's continued financial support, but otherwise, I would speak to him only on social occasions related to town functions.

I was still sitting at the circulation desk when Wade came in.

"What's up, boss? You look worried."

"Didn't Juliet tell you what happened last night?"

Wade set his lunch box down on the desk. "Yeah. Willow wigged out on the new board member. Big deal."

"The mayor called a half-hour ago and wants to see me. I have a feeling it's related to the company I keep. Graham thinks librarians should be ninety-year-old spinsters with twenty cats and a bun."

Wade waved my worry aside. "I'm sure it's nothing. Maybe he wants to discuss something for Founder's Day."

I stood up and grabbed my purse from my desk drawer. "It's slow, so I'm going to grab a cup of coffee and head to town hall. You okay on your own?"

Wade looked around at the space. "I'll try to hold down the fort with all these demanding patrons." He glanced at our sole patron with his nose buried in the newspaper. "They might get rowdy."

I walked down the street to Nellie Jo's. I needed caffeine and one of her fattening chocolate croissants. It would make me feel one hundred percent better, I was sure.

After I placed my order, I sat at the counter on one of the cushioned stools. Nellie brought my coffee in a to-go cup with a warm chocolate croissant wrapped in paper.

"What's wrong?" she asked.

"How can you tell?"

"You only order chocolate croissants when you're stressed. Otherwise, you're a scone girl." She rested her elbows on the counter and eyed me. "Is it the murder investigation?"

I sighed. "Yes. No. Maybe. It's everything. I have a new board member who's the morality police. Juliet threatened to cancel the wedding. There's a bare spot in my backyard that was supposed to be a gazebo. And now, the mayor wants to see me in twenty minutes."

Nellie picked up a cloth and wiped the already spotless counter. "That's a lot on anybody's plate, but you know what?"

"What?"

"They can't take away your birthday." Nellie gave me a beatific smile.

I laughed. Nellie Jo's words of wisdom were profound and funny at the same time. "You're right. It might be nothing." I reached into my purse for my wallet and my hands touched the keyring and key I had found last night. I pulled it out and dangled it in front of her. "Any idea what this key might be for?"

She took it from my outstretched hand. "This looks like one of them keyrings they used to give you when you opened up a bank account. Of course, nowadays you get fancy coffee mugs and pens."

"I think you're right. Mom has an old keyring from the bank here in town. She keeps the key to the lawnmower on it."

Nellie peered at the faint writing. She lifted her

glasses up and rested them on her forehead. "It looks like this here is from the First National Bank of Burlington." She put her glasses back on her nose. "I bet that's a key to a safe deposit box. Looks like the one I got to keep my important documents in at the bank."

I took the key back from her. She might be right. I would have to make a trip to the bank in Burlington to find out, but first I needed to see the mayor.

I paid Nellie for the coffee and the croissant and hurried down the sidewalk to the town hall. I took a big bite and warm chocolate filled my mouth. Some people wanted liquid courage, but for me, chocolate and carbs always did the trick.

I was sitting outside of the mayor's office a few minutes later. The hard wooden chairs were not helping to soothe my nerves. His secretary had buzzed him to let him know I'd arrived. I felt like I had been called to the principal's office, not that I knew anything about that. Juliet had been a frequent flier when we were in high school. She had always been outspoken in her opinions and her fashion choices. She flouted the rules with regularity.

Mayor James opened the door. "Phee, come on in."

"Mayor, good to see you." I followed him in and sat primly on the edge of the chair in front of his desk. I smoothed my skirt.

"I'm sure you're wondering why I wanted to see you."

"Yes, sir. Is there something I can help with?

The library staff and I are always willing to-"

He held his hand up to stop me. "First, call me Monty. I've known you and your family for years. I might be the mayor, but I put my pants on the same way as everyone else."

For a moment, I had a flash of the mayor in boxers, and I felt a little awkward and a little ill. I quickly trashed the image from my brain.

"I wanted to talk to you about a concern raised by one of my constituents," he said. "You seem to have gotten yourself into a bit of trouble with a body showing up in your backyard and now you're on the scene right after someone killed Craig Muldean."

A rock sat in my stomach. *Graham Lawson and his pious perfection.* "Mayor, I mean Monty, someone buried Dean Winters in my backyard before I was even born. As for Craig, it was an unhappy coincidence I went to visit him." I decided it was not time to be timid. "Actually, Monty, weren't you friends with Dean Winters and Craig Muldean when you were young? My mom says she's known you for years and you all used to be friends. You took photographs of the band, right?"

Monty clasped his hands together on the desk and leaned forward. "I was, and I have to say it shocked and saddened when I learned it was Dean. To be honest, I was always on the fringe of that group of kids. They were a little too wild for me."

My mom wild? I knew it had been the seventies and everyone was still doing the peace, love, and happiness gig, but I had a difficult time imagining my college professor mom as wild. "Wild? In what ways?"

103

"Dean had a reputation with women and there were rumors he skirted on the edge of the law sometimes. It surprised me when your mother went out with him. I had always hoped…" He stopped and leaned back. "Sheila had a huge crush on Dean, and it caused a bit of a rift between your mom and her. I don't think your mother knew that Sheila had puppy dog eyes every time Dean showed up. Kid stuff, you know."

"Teenage girls are known to have crushes," I agreed, but I thought about my mom and how she said they had been close before that summer.

"It was a long time ago, and we've all built good lives here in Miller's Cove. It's a shame about Dean and Craig, but I'm strongly suggesting you steer clear of criminals and crime scenes."

"I will try my best."

Monty stood up, signaling the meeting was over.

"You know Graham Lawson, correct?" I asked as I stood.

Monty hesitated. "Yes, I know Graham. He's an asset to the community. He and his church members actively work to improve Miller's Cove. Graham is generous with both church funds and its resources for members of this community."

The way Monty talked made me suspect Graham gave a generous donation to his mayoral campaign. "Was he the one who complained?"

"Now, Phee, I can't betray a confidence. I don't want you to worry about it. I've said what needed to be said, and the matter is closed." He walked to the door and opened it.

My cue to leave. "Thank you for your time, Mayor."

"Monty."

I nodded and hurried out of the office. I needed to talk to my mom again. There was something she was hiding, and I was determined to find out what it was.

Chapter Fifteen

I called Juliet on my way back to the library. I wouldn't interrogate Mom on my own again. Juliet might clamp fuzzy handcuffs on me and lock me in my house if she felt like I was being too rough, but I needed her support.

"Monty said that Dean Winters was a ladies' man and a little wild back in the day," I said.

"Monty?"

"Mayor James. He called me in to read me the riot act over my association with criminal activity. But I don't care about that right now. I'm more concerned that Mom was a wild woman and not the person we think she is," I said.

"Mom volunteers for Ladies Auxiliary, for Pete's sake. She's about as wild as a houseplant," Juliet said.

"Regardless, I think we need to talk to her."

A horn honked behind me, and I turned to look.

"Watch out!"

I slammed into a large, immoveable object. I bounced like a woman on a bungee cord and landed on my butt. "Ouch!" I looked up and saw Lu glaring down at me, rubbing her belly. "Are you okay? Is the baby okay?"

"I'm fine. My gun belt protected her."

"Her? It's a girl." I stood up and brushed off my skirt.

"Her. Him. It's just an expression," Lu said, eyes sliding away from mine. "What are you up to?

You look guilty."

"Nothing. Talking to Juliet. How's the investigation going? Am I going to have a wedding?"

"I don't know why you can't have one now. The crime scene's cleared. Your guys can come back and build the gazebo," she said.

"Juliet says the spirits cursed the impending nuptials. She refuses to make plans or let me do anything until the spirits tell her it's okay."

Lu rolled her eyes. "Ridiculous. Spirits are a load of hooey."

"I totally agree, but you know how Juls is."

Lu squinted and took a step forward to peer over my shoulder. Then she shook her head. "Nah. Couldn't be."

"What?" I turned and looked over my shoulder.

"Anthony. I thought I saw him, but there's no way he would come back to Miller's Cove." I could have sworn a look of sadness crossed her face.

I gave a guilty laugh. "Anthony? Here in Miller's Cove? Doubtful."

Lu gave me the hairy eyeball. She was intimidating for such a petite woman with a beach ball-sized belly. "You're hiding something. I just don't know about what. Give me time. I'll ferret it out."

My eyes grew wide. Oh, crap! I was on Lu's radar. I would have to stay out of her way. "Not up to anything. Gotta go. See ya." I scurried away before she could interrogate me further. Now I knew how the mouse felt when the tomcat played with it before pouncing.

Back at the library, I was relieved to see it was busy. Wade gave me a harried look. Cris Dowd, the town storyteller pinned him to the circulation desk. Her stories weren't interesting or even on point with anyone else in the conversation. She just like to tell long stories.

I took pity on him and shooed him away from the desk. "Hey, Cris. How's everything?"

"Did you hear about the Craig's murder?" Cris asked.

"I was the one who found the body," I said. Clearly, Cris didn't listen to the gossip that closely.

"Golly. Really? That must have been terrifying. I wondered what was going on. You know I live two houses down from him. I heard a loud commotion that made me too scared to come out of my house."

Aha! An ear witness, and according to several crime shows I watched, this might be admissible in court if she identified someone from their voice.

"What sort of commotion?" I asked, trying for casual, knowing Cris might digress into a story about one of her many cats.

"Well, I heard some shouting, and I said to Miss Mittens, that's my calico, that someone was in a tizzy."

"Could you tell who it was? Man or woman?"

"Definitely two men. I couldn't hear what they were yelling because I had the television on to the morning game shows. Maximillian loves *The Price is Right*. I didn't think I'd like it after Bob Barker left, but Max doesn't care. He loves the buzzers and spinning wheel to reach a dollar. He'll sit and stare at the screen for the entire hour. Do you have any cats?"

"One. Did you see anyone at Craig's?" I asked. I said a silent prayer that she would stay focused for a few more questions. Almost across the finish line. Wade smirked at me from across the room.

"No. It was close to the final showcase, and I hate to miss it. You know they give away cars and campers and stuff at the end. Why I would love–"

"I've seen the show. Anything else you can remember?"

Cris stood for a moment and tapped her chin with her finger. "Now that I think about it, one thing was odd. I took my trash out later and someone had tossed their trash into my can. Can you believe it? The nerve of some people. I think it's the new guy that moved in down the street. He's from somewhere out west. You know the kind."

"Not really. I think people are the same all over. Did they pick up your trash yet? Can I stop by and see what they threw away in there?" I had a hunch.

"Now, why would you want to do that?" Cris laughed. "I'm sure you've got your own garbage if you like to dig through stuff. I watched a show once where everyone dumpster dives to create art."

"I can't tell you why, but I really need to see what they threw into your trash can. You've known me a long time, Cris. Would I do anything weird?"

Cris shook her hand and chuckled. "It's still there and you're welcome to it. Best hurry though. Trash pickup is tomorrow morning and they come early."

"Great. I'll stop by this afternoon. Thanks. It was good chatting with you. I'd better get back to work. Those books won't shelve themselves." I pointed at the three lone books on the shelving cart.

Cris waved goodbye and ambled out of the door. She was a nice lady, but quirky. She also had more cats than anyone I knew. I worried that one day we would see her on one of the animal hoarding shows, but Cris made sure any orphaned kittens got their shots and were neutered. She also found them loving homes. She operated an informal cat rescue for the town.

Time dragged by after that as I watched the clock. I would swing by Cris's place to dig through her trash, then stop by to see Juliet. When five o'clock came, I snatched up my purse and waved goodbye to Wade and Olivia, our evening clerk.

At Cris's house, I spent a few minutes admiring and petting her cats. It was a small price to pay since I loved animals anyway, but I was impatient to see if my hunch was correct.

Cris led me through her house stuffed with old paperbacks, newspapers, and more cat trees than I could count. She pointed to the trash can outside her back door.

"You're welcome to it. Could you do me a favor? Could you push it to the curb for me when you're done? The bursitis in my shoulder has been acting up." She moved her arm around and winced. "Doctor wants to give me a shot, but I don't like them."

I interrupted her before she could go into minute detail of her various ailments. I could catalog her

110

doctor's visits in my sleep. Today, I was too eager to get to her trash. "I'd be happy to, Cris. It's the least I can do."

I hurried down her back steps and lifted the lid off her trash can. When I did, I reeled back from the smell of old cans of cat food and spoiled milk. This better be worth it. I tried to remember when I had a tetanus shot. I reached in and pulled the bag on top out of the can. A small white grocery bag lay at the bottom. I leaned in and could barely reach it with the tips of my fingers. I balanced on my tiptoes and stretched further. With a sudden shift, I grabbed the bag just as my body plunged face first into the trash can.

"Criminy!" I yelled and instantly regretted opening my mouth as the wetness of leaked garbage touched my lips and face. The trash can tumbled over with me and I crawled backwards out of it. I stood up with the small white bag clutched in my fist.

I gulped in clean air and used the end of my shirt to wipe the crud and goo from my lips and face. Without hesitation, I tore open the bag. Inside, I found a bowling trophy with Craig Muldean's name etched on a brass plate on the front. It was covered with something brown and crusty that I knew right away was blood.

Careful not to touch the contents, I laid the bag down on the ground. So much for avoiding Lu.

Twenty minutes later, Lu relieved me of my evidence. She stayed well away from me since she claimed I smelled like an old tuna sandwich that had sat in the sun too long. I didn't take umbrage at the description. I felt like one, too.

"I thought you were staying out of it," Lu said. She placed the trophy in an evidence bag. She removed her own gloves and tucked them in her back pocket. "How did you even think to come here?"

"Cris visited the library and mentioned she'd heard an altercation at Craig's house the morning of the murder. She also complained that someone had dumped something into her trash. The guy I saw running away was heading in this direction. It was a hunch."

"It was a good hunch," Lu said. "It will take a week or two, but I've got a theory that it's Craig's blood on that trophy. Hopefully, we can pull some prints, too."

After Lu told me it was okay to leave, I hopped in Velma and headed straight to Juliet's. When I pulled up to the sidewalk, I saw Wade's Jeep. Good. Three brains were better than one.

"What in the goddess's good name happened to you?" Juliet wrinkled her nose.

"It's a long story."

"You need a shower. I'll find something you can wear. I can't talk to you because you're making my eyes burn." She shooed me to her bathroom.

Fifteen minutes later, I had scrubbed the stink away and smelled of Juliet's patchouli-scented soap and shampoo. She found me a pair of too long yoga pants and an oversized shirt. I felt like a little kid wearing her mother's clothes. At least, I no longer attracted the neighborhood cats with my stench.

I told Juliet all about my adventure into the depths of local trashcans and discovering the murder weapon.

"That was pretty smart of you," Juliet said.

"Thanks. I am the brains of our family."

"Actually, if you were smart, you would have tipped the can over considering you're only about three feet tall on your best day," Juliet said with a smart aleck grin.

"You two are hilarious," Wade said, stepping between us before our verbal sparring increased. "Tell me why the mayor wanted to see you. It was so busy earlier at work, so I never asked you what happened."

"I already told Juls, but basically, Graham called the mayor and complained about my lack of morality."

"You?" Wade spit out his beer. "You're the most strait-laced person I know."

"It's the whole dead body in the backyard that has Graham up in arms," I said. "I told Monty I would leave detecting to the professionals."

"Which means us because we're the professionals, just not police professionals," Juliet said.

I rolled my eyes. Juliet could split a hair so much that we could make it into a fur coat. "I love my job, and I'm not willing to lose it."

I held up a finger when she sputtered a protest. "However, I see nothing wrong with asking a few gentle questions if we run into a few parties who may or may not be suspects."

"Excellent. Who are our suspects?" Juliet leaned on her elbows. "Anyone at the top of the list?"

"Funny you should ask," I said. "Our biggest

suspect for the first murder is someone we know well."

"Who?" Wade asked.

"Mom."

Chapter Sixteen

"Mom?" Juliet squealed. "Are you out of your ever-loving mind? Clearly, the stress of my wedding and finding Craig murdered has scrambled your brains."

If I could have scowled any deeper at my sister, I would have. Instead, I waited until her huffing and puffing over my mental state ended before I spoke again. "Regardless of if you want to hear it or not, our mother had a relationship with *our* victim. I have proof."

"But it's Mom. You know, the person who gave you life."

"I found a photograph with Mom and the dead guy from my yard. They dated. She had a romantic relationship with him. She was one of the last people to see him alive. If we're professionals, we need to put her on the suspect list."

Juliet's eyes narrowed, then turned mischievous. "She's going to write you out of the will. I'll be the favorite daughter from now on. Besides, we know she dated Dean. How does she become suspect number one?"

I thought about how to phrase my next statement without sounding like a horrible daughter. "Mom bent the truth when she told me about Dean. She said it wasn't serious, but according to people who knew them at the time, they were serious enough that people thought they would marry."

Juliet let out a raspberry. "People in this town

gossip. Gossip is not fact. You need to do better than that."

"People do gossip, but I think we need to know why they argued and if they had talked about marriage. The police are going to ask her the same questions. Why not ferret out the answers from her before they do?"

Juliet scowled at me, but I waited and let her stew on my words. Finally, she said, "Let's go now and get it over with, but I'm driving. I want to make a fast getaway if we make her angry."

"I'll stay here. There's no way I want to be a party to that conversation," Wade said.

"Chicken, but I don't blame you. We'll be back in an hour," Juliet said, then gave him a quick peck on the lips. "Wish us luck."

"You'll need more than luck," Wade said under his breath.

"What?" Juliet asked. She rummaged through her yoga bag for her car keys and wasn't looking at us.

I glared at him and did a chopping motion against my neck. "He said good luck."

She raised her keys in triumph. "Aha! Let's go."

***

It only took us ten minutes to reach our parents' home on the outskirts of Miller's Cove. Juliet killed the engine to her Karmann Ghia, and the two of us sat staring at the front door. I figured Juliet was thinking about waiting for me to get out of the car before firing up the engine and burning rubber as she escaped and left me to fend for myself.

"Maybe they aren't home," she said.

"Her car is in the driveway. She's home."

"She's probably busy grading."

"It's spring break," I said. "Now, stop making excuses and let's get it done and over with. The sooner we strike her off our list of suspects, the sooner we can concentrate on other people."

Resigned, Juliet tucked her car keys in her pocket and opened her car door. Only once she had stepped out of the car did I open my door. The two of us trudged to the house. I knocked then opened the door. No one locked their houses when they were home in Miller's Cove. It was only recently that my parents started to lock their doors at night. I did because I lived in town and knew some of the visitors to the summer cottages were sometimes unsavory characters, but my parents still lived in the seventies and eighties when crime was nonexistent in town.

"Mom? Where are you?" I called.

Our dog Hamlet let out a woof of greeting from where he lay in his dog bed. He didn't bother to get up. An Irish Setter, his red fur showed a few patches of white around his eyes and muzzle. I walked over and patted his head. His tail did a quick swish before he closed his eyes to finish his nap.

"I'm in the kitchen," Mom answered.

Juliet and I looked at each other then back at the door, but we came with a purpose and our mission needed to be completed. "Come on," I hissed. "You're

117

her favorite. You ask her."

Juliet rolled her eyes and said, "I want to stay her favorite. Your idea. You ask."

"Fine."

I strode into the kitchen with Juliet trailing behind me. "Hey, Mom. Where's Dad?"

My mother was at the counter with her hands elbow deep in bread dough. She pointed with her chin. "In the den watching some inane reality show. I'm making bread to go with the corn chowder I plan to make tomorrow."

Our mother made the best food when she wasn't on the warpath to make our father eat healthier. When his cholesterol or blood pressure was too high, she switched from comfort food to tofu. It wasn't a good change. I usually checked with Dad to determine which way the menu might be before agreeing to eat at their house. I like healthy food, sometimes, but I love breads and a variety of carbs.

"I'm going to say hi to Dad," Juliet said and turned to leave, but I grabbed her arm and glared.

Mom stopped mixing the dough and her eyes went from my face to Juliet's and back again. I looked away. "You girls are up to something. I can always tell. Phee never makes eye contact, and Juliet finds an excuse to leave the room. It's how your father and I always caught you when you misbehaved. Have a seat while I wash my hands."

We quickly obeyed and sat down at the kitchen table. I mouthed to Juliet, "You ask."

She gave a violent shake of her head and

mouthed. "Not me."

Mom turned off the water and dried her hands. She sat down next to me. "What's on your mind?"

"Phee has something she wants to ask you?" Juliet blurted, then gave me a smug grin.

I sighed. "Mom, I wanted to ask you some more about Dean Winters. The police are going to want to talk to you and your relationship."

Mom frowned. "Why? It was such a long time ago, and I was a teenager. It was a summer romance, and Lu already gave me the third degree." She shot me a meaningful look that told me I needed to mind my p's and q's.

I picked at the edges of my fingernails, not wanting to look at her. "Here's the thing. I found that photograph at Mr. Muldean's house. It fell on the floor, and I picked it up."

"You tampered with a crime scene?" Mom asked, her frown deepening.

I grimaced. "I guess. It was the shock of the murder and seeing a photograph with you and Dean. I wasn't thinking."

"How many times have I told you girls to think before you act. If I've said it once, I've said it a thousand times."

I finally looked at her. "I know, and I'm sorry. I turned it over to the police. They're going to want to see what information you might have and possibly anyone who may have had a grudge against Dean."

"We were kids, Phee. Why would anyone hold a grudge against any of us? A teenage prank? This isn't one of your mystery novels. It's the real world," Mom said.

I gritted my teeth. I wanted to shout that I wasn't a teenager, either so I knew it wasn't a mystery novel. Instead, I took a deep, calming breath like Juliet taught me during meditation class. "Mom, I know that you were a teenager, but from what I understand, everyone else was older."

Mom looked up at the ceiling, and I saw her counting on her fingers. When she was done, she said, "You're right. Sheila was only a year older than me. She graduated late because she had a late birthday. She was six when she started kindergarten. The guys were all in their early twenties. To be honest, I'm surprised your grandparents allowed me to spend as much time with Dean as they did."

Now we're getting somewhere. The nut finally cracked a little. Now to get at the meat of the matter. "Mom, you showed me the photographs of you and your friends, but that's only a snapshot of a moment. What else was going on that summer? What were they like? Any bad romances? Arguments?"

Mom went to the sink and grabbed a dishrag. She slowly wiped the counter. Juliet and I stayed silent, an unspoken agreement to let our mother take her time to answer. When she finally spoke, her voice was quiet and tired. "It was such a long time ago. A lifetime. When I left for college, I started a new chapter in my life and left all the old grudges and bickering behind."

"Mom, tell us how you met Dean," Juliet said. I shot her a grateful look. I knew I would need reinforcements, and I was right.

Mom smiled. "Dean was handsome in a bad boy way. Sort of like your father."

"Dad?" Juliet and I asked in unison.

She laughed. "Your father wasn't always an English professor. He was a person before he was your dad. He really filled out that leather jacket he used to wear and his jeans... well, all the girls in my dorm were crazy about him."

I shuddered a little at the idea of my dad as a sex symbol. Some clues were worth keeping buried. "And Dean?" I prompted.

"Dean wasn't from a nice family like your dad. He grew up hard, and he had a lot of anger. His dad was killed in Vietnam when he was a baby, so it was just he and his mom. If I'm remembering correctly, she was a waitress at an all-night truck stop. I met her once. She was a nice lady but looked older than her years. The two of them lived in a rough part of Burlington, and money was always tight. Dean had big dreams and would always tell me he wouldn't be poor again. He would do whatever it took to get ahead."

Juliet nodded. "I know some people like that. Ruled by the dollar. They spend their lives trying to get ahead, and they don't care who they step on to get there."

Mom stopped cleaning the counters and sat back down next to us. She leaned forward. "That's just it. It's why we wouldn't have lasted beyond the summer. He didn't know how to just slow down and breathe for a moment. Always scheming and wheeling and dealing to

121

get their band a new gig. I met him in late April, and I think I was more flattered by all of his compliments rather than by his personality. Dean was good looking and charming. He could charm the pants off—"

I held up my hand. "Stop! Don't go there."

"Well, I certainly didn't go there. It's part of the reason we fought that night and broke up. He wanted more than I was willing to give. And he wanted me to ditch college and go to California with him the next day."

Juliet got up and rummaged in the kitchen cabinets. She came back with a bag of gingersnap cookies. "Anyone want a glass of milk. I think I need the sugar jolt to get through the rest of this story."

We all wanted cookies and milk. It took me back to when we were teenagers and would come home from a night out with friends or a boy, and Mom would be sitting at the kitchen table reading a book. She would pour us a glass of milk and have a plate of cookies. We would spend the next half hour sharing the highlights of our night. Now that I'm older, I realize not everyone had this charmed life. Juliet and I were fortunate to have such wonderful parents.

"So, he wanted you to go to California. You said he'd been talking about it, so it must not have come as a shock," I said. I dipped my gingersnap into the cold glass of milk and counted to ten. I had cookie dunking down to an exact science. Too short and the cookie was still hard. Too long and the cookie disintegrated into the glass or was mush in your mouth.

Mom chewed her cookie, her eyes thoughtful.

"Thinking back on it, I realize it was a shock. Dean planned to go to California in 1980. He said it would take him a whole year to save up. That's why it was such a surprise that he planned to leave the next day."

"Why the change?" Juliet said, sporting a small milk mustache which on her made her look cute. On me, I'd look like a slob.

"I don't know. He said he had to get out of town fast, but he wouldn't tell me why."

I added this fact to the growing list of clues I had in my head. "Who knew you had a fight that night?" I asked.

"Everybody in the band. And Sheila, of course."

"Nobody called Dean out over ditching Miller's Cove and heading to California."

She slowly shook her head, then stopped. "Wait. I think Craig knew because he said something to Dean. He said something like he guessed Robin Hood's Merry Band of Thieves would be a little bit smaller."

"That's odd," Juliet said.

"Craig always joked and said they were the Four Musketeers or silly stuff like that. Dean would get angry and tell him to shut up."

Everything my mother just told us swirled around in my head. Had Dean Winters made someone so angry he feared for his life? If so, who?

Chapter Seventeen

I munched on another cookie as I thought about Mom's revelation that Dean wanted her to leave town with him the next day. Clearly, he never left since he ended up in my backyard. What happened between the time he and Mom argued, and the time he died?

"Wait a second. It isn't cheap to go to California. Did he have a car? An airplane ticket? How did he plan to get there?" Juliet asked.

"Dean had a motorcycle. That thing was his pride and joy. I loved riding on the back of it. Hair flying in the wind. Girls, there's nothing like the back of a Harley to make you feel free."

"Whoa. You didn't wear a helmet? Aren't you the one who grounded me for forgetting my bike helmet one time?" Juliet arched her brow at Mom. "I'm shocked and appalled, Mother."

"It was a different time," Mom answered, staring Juliet down over the rim of her glasses. Juliet lost that staring contest. Mom was the champion of the "death stare."

"First, what happened to his motorcycle? Second, where did he get the money? Finally, why the sudden hurry to get out of Miller's Cove?" I ticked off the questions on my fingers. "The cops are going to want to know the answers to these questions, and they'll probably have more."

"I'm an open book," Mom said. "And I have no answers to any of those questions. As soon as he asked me to go to California the next day, we argued. I had no plans to abandon my dreams of college and career to chase after a cute guy in a band."

"Even if they had a cool name like The Screaming Goats," Juliet said.

I wasn't ready to give up so easily. "What about the other people in the photographs? What were they like? How were they around Dean?"

"Sheila liked him," Mom said. "They had a lot in common. Both grew up poor and wanted a better life. I'd find them hanging out talking about their dreams for the future. Now that I look back on it, they were a better fit than Dean and I ever were."

"Sheila Dawes? The sheriff's wife? Our Sheila who taught our Sunday School class when we were kids?" Juliet asked.

Mom nodded. "She and I were best friends as teenagers. Something changed that summer. There was an odd tension between everyone. I thought I was cool hanging out with the band, and I thought Sheila felt the same. We planned on having our best summer before we left for college, but she got hurt and lost her scholarship. When she wasn't angry, she was wild."

My eyebrows shot up at the image of Sheila being angry or wild. "It doesn't sound like her."

"She's not like that now, but she was that summer. She had a track scholarship to the University of Florida. Full ride. She was an amazing athlete back then," Mom said.

"What happened?" Juliet stopped dunking her cookie long enough to ask.

"She tore a tendon or something one day when she fell. I was her best friend, and I told her I would help her. She told me there was nothing someone like me could do to help her. It changed our friendship, and we weren't as close." Mom looked sad. "We still hung out every day, but it wasn't the same. Once she recovered from the surgery to her tendon, she went crazy. Sheila flirted with the guys and would drink even though we were underage. To be honest, I'm surprised she straightened up and got it together."

"So, she didn't go to college?" I reached into my purse and pulled out my phone. Clint needed to know that I was at my parent's house since it was my turn to cook. We took turns several nights a week cooking dinner. His meals were always interesting. He either ordered delivery or made breakfast for dinner. It was a meal he made like five-star chef.

"Sheila didn't have money for a university. Her dad was a handyman and did odd jobs. For a while that summer, she would say she could sort it all out, but then she ended up going to the community college in Burlington. That's where she met Jaime. They fell in love and got married. Once Jaime completed his training at the police academy, they moved here, and he got a job as a deputy."

"So, a happy ending for Sheila," Juliet said, wiping the crumbs from the table into her hand. She put them into the trashcan and grabbed all of our glasses.

I tapped out my message to Clint. As I went to swipe my phone to check for any other messages, I accidentally clicked on my photos and saw the picture of the letters I had seen at Craig's house. I realized that the letter was written to Lola and signed by Craig. Boring details of a bachelor's life running a hardware store. I opened up the picture and showed it to Mom. "Who is Lola Richardson?"

Mom shook her head. "No idea."

"But I do," Dad said from the doorway. "I didn't want to interrupt the hen party, so I stayed in the den."

"That's a sexist thing to say, Dad." Juliet scowled. She didn't enjoy being pigeonholed into a role as a woman. "Hen party."

"I knew that would get a rise out of you, chicken," Dad said, as he ruffled her hair. He kissed her on the cheek. "Wanted to make sure you weren't giving up the good fight yet."

"Never." Juliet did a fist pump into the air.

I rolled my eyes and gave her a pointed look. She was moving us off topic. She was supposed to be Pepper Anderson, but she was Gloria Steinem today. Usually, I am one hundred percent behind her, but I needed her to focus. "As you were saying, Dad, who was Lola Richardson?"

"Craig's younger sister. Well, stepsister, I should say. His dad married her mom. She was about ten or fifteen years younger than him and didn't live here." He came over and rested his hand on the back of Mom's chair. "Lola was a nickname." He tapped his index finger on his chin. "Nope. Her real name was on the tip of my tongue, but now it's gone. Is it important?"

My shoulders slumped in defeat. "No. So these letters weren't important. Just letters between brother and sister."

"Craig would talk about her sometimes when we went fishing or had a cup of coffee together. He said they used to be close, but she got married and Craig didn't approve of her husband. They had a falling out and hadn't talked or seen each other since the early eighties."

Mom clucked her tongue. "It's a shame that families fall apart over silly things. Now, it's too late for Lola to have a relationship with Craig."

Juliet grabbed me around my shoulders and gave me a wet, sloppy kiss on my cheek. "Ew. What did you do that for?"

"I wanted to make sure you know I will always be there for you. Our sisterhood will never fall apart. If we survived those hideous bedazzled ski masks and almost getting eaten by an alligator together, nothing will tear us apart."

I patted her arm. "Ah, I love you, too, Juls. Now give me a napkin so I can wipe your cooties off."

"You know who you should talk to?" Dad asked. "Mrs. Lancaster."

"Ah, crud biscuits!" I smacked my palm against my forehead. "I promised her I would see her, and I never did."

Juliet gave a low whistle. "Way to go, sis. Make the nicest and most influential woman in town upset with you."

I groaned. *One more person in town to add to*

PERMANENTLY DELETED

my growing list of people I displeased.

Chapter Eighteen

Juliet dropped me off at my van, and I cruised through the streets of my hometown, lost in thought. This town was in my blood the way adventure or travel pumped through other people. A natural homebody, it saddened me to think someone whose face I looked at over the circulation desk might be a killer. I don't know how the sheriff and his deputies did it every day. I knew that Clint knew many townspeople's dirty little secrets, but he never shared. Sometimes, he might mention an incident. However, he was careful to exclude names.

As a librarian, I knew some secrets, too. For example, I knew that Mr. Carpuccio's wife checked out bodice-ripper romances, or as I liked to call them, bonnet-rippers because it involved the plot revolved around Amish romance. Clara Millhaven asked me regularly if I had added more "romances" like a certain book with many shades of gray in the title. She always used air quotes and gave me a knowing smile. I bought a broad range of genres and tried to please everyone, but there were some niches that I gritted my teeth when I allocated a portion of my budget to their purchase. Oh, well. I was director of a library meant to serve everyone equally, regardless of their taste in literature.

The thought of Clara's penchant for erotic romance made me do a mental head thump. What would Graham Lawson think of those books in our collection? Would he be like a recent county school system in Virginia whose board member had called for the actual burning of books? I shuddered. Perhaps it was time to apply to a branch of the Burlington library system. The prospect of sitting across from Graham Lawson for the next two years until his seat was vacant again filled me with dread.

As I turned down a side street, I saw a light shining in the old clock repair shop. It had closed a few years ago when Sidney Portman and his wife, Charlotte, retired while they were still young enough to cruise around the country in an RV. Business had slowed, and the few people who still used his services were content to drive into Burlington for their needs. Someone must have bought the building finally. Curious, I slowed Velma to a crawl and looked to see who the new tenant might be. Rolls of paper covered the windows, but light shone through a small crack. In the alley next to the building, I spotted Anthony's car.

"What in the world is he doing?" I eased Velma into a parking spot opposite the shop and killed the engine. Anthony had been making himself scarce since he launched Operation Baby, as I called it. I quickly crossed the street and rapped on the glass door. "Anthony, is that you? It's me. Let me in?"

"Whose me?" Anthony's voice sounded muffled.

"Come on. It's Phee. Let me in." I knocked on the glass door again. A minute later, I heard some shuffling and the lock being turned. Expecting to see Anthony, I let out a scream at the mask-covered man in front of me.

Anthony lifted it from his face. "Sh! Get inside

131

before anyone sees you."

My heart pounded in my chest as I slipped inside. He locked the door behind me. "What's with the terrifying mask?"

Anthony yanked it off his head. "It's a respirator mask. I've got horrible dust allergies and that back room has a layer about a foot deep. It's going to take me a month to get this place cleaned up."

I looked around. He had replaced the boring white walls of the clock shop with a bold shade of navy blue with dark cherry wood molding. The name Ziegfried Security Services was painted in discreet gold lettering on the back wall. A curved desk stained to match the molding occupied the center of the room. "What is all of this?"

"It's my new business," Anthony said. "I will offer security services to the businesses and homes in the area. It's a business this town has been begging for since the increase in crime the past few years. Look at what happened to you? If you had an excellent security system with cameras, you would have been much safer."

"I live with a man who carries a gun and a badge," I said, giving him a wry grin.

He waved his finger at me. "Fair enough, but are you going to share Clint with the rest of the frightened women in town and absentee cottage owners?"

He had a good point. "I get it, but what about the senator and his campaign?"

"When I called the senator and told him about

Lu, he said not to hesitate. I've trained Gary Sneed, a junior campaign aide, for the past year. It's a great opportunity for Gary to shine and prove himself. Plus, with videoconferencing, I can answer questions he might have. I have to do this to win Lu back, Phee. She's the one." Anthony ran his fingers through his hair.

I laughed and reached over and smoothed it back down. "How many times have I told you that you look like a red-headed hedgehog when you do that? Are you sure you're ready to give up your career for Lu?"

He stared at me, his eyes intense. "Yes. I would move the stars in the sky for that woman. You know what I mean, don't you? Look at you and Clint."

Yeah. Look at us. Too scared to commit. I pushed the thought from my head. "Is this where you've been staying?"

"Nope. I bought a house, too. It's a fixer upper, but it had the best yard for a kid. Space for a swing set and a dog. Heck, I could put in a small basketball court for him, or her, if they wanted. The owner's already moved out, so he's letting me rent until I close."

I let out a low whistle. "Boy, you are taking a risk. Quit your job. Starting a new business. Remodeling a house. It's barely been a week."

Anthony looked at his feet. "I may have withheld some information. I made a trip back here a few weeks ago." At my shocked expression, he hurried on before I could interrupt. "It was literally a day trip. I found this place for sale online, and I contacted the real estate agent. It was a done deal. I could have faxed my signature, but I wanted to see if I could talk to Lu."

"So, you knew she was pregnant?"

He shook his head. "No. I knew Lu was the woman I'm meant to marry. I didn't plan to move here so quickly. It was supposed to be my new path once the campaign was over, but the baby sped things up."

"What if it all goes belly up?"

His look grew even more serious. "It won't. I am not a quitter. Besides, even if Lu tells me she hates me and never wants to see my face again, my child deserves to have a father in their life. Not some weekend dad who takes them out for fast food and crappy movies. No, Phee, if Lu doesn't want me, I'm still a dad. That is everything to me."

Tears welled in my eyes. Dang, this man was a keeper. Why couldn't Lu see that? "You're going to be the best father and husband. Lu's got her reasons, but she's keeping them to herself. You're a good man, Anthony. She'll see that."

He laid his hand on my shoulder. "Thanks, Phee. I'm fine if she doesn't. I made peace with my good and bad qualities years ago."

A loud banging on the door startled us. "Concord County police. Open up."

The voice was loud but contained a hint of mama bear. "Holy guacamole. It's Lu." I looked for a rear exit.

Anthony's face morphed into a whole range of emotions. It started with alarmed but settled on resolved. "No time like the present. Wish me luck." He went and turned the lock on the door.

One-hundred and fifty pounds of pregnant cop charged through the door, hand on her gun. When she saw Anthony, she stopped and looked around in confusion. When she spotted me, she scowled. "I should have known something was up. You never can keep a secret."

Holding up my hands, I said, "I'm innocent this time. I need to get home to Clint." Giving Lu a wide berth, I mouthed "good luck" to Anthony over her shoulder with a thumbs up. As I closed the door behind me, all I heard was the empty sound of silence. I only hoped it was a good sign.

Chapter Nineteen

At home, I found Clint asleep on the couch with Watson and Fritz curled up together in the corner on one dog bed. Ferdinand sat like a regal sphinx on the top of a bookshelf, surveying his domain. Although I tried to be quiet, Clint still woke up. "Hey, stranger. I wondered if you were going to make it home. Did you eat?"

"Cookies at Mom's," I admitted. I dropped my purse on the chair and leaned down to give him a kiss. "I have so much to tell you."

"The same. I saved you two slices of the pizza I picked up on my way home. After the day I had, I didn't want either of us to have to cook. Let's go heat it up and talk."

He led me down the hall to the kitchen, our fingers intertwined. The comfort of his presence melted the stress of the past few days. Maybe the two of us needed to take a trip somewhere alone. No crime. No library board members. Just a romantic getaway for two for the weekend. It sounded marvelous.

I stuck the pizza slices into the toaster oven to reheat them. A microwave would be faster, but I hated a soggy, chewy crust. I was a thin crust girl, but Clint was a thick crust lover, so when he bought the pizza, it was his way. It worked out alright since nine times out of ten, it was me choosing pizza. I could swallow a ridiculously thick crust for the sake of a relationship once in a blue moon.

He poured us both a glass of Cabernet and then

sat at the table. "You go first."

"Are you sure? My day was like herding mice towards a cathouse." I took a sip of wine and allowed the leathery, smooth liquid to rest a moment on my tongue. "This is an excellent wine."

"I picked it up last week last time I went with Wade to his prosthetic guy. I forgot I had it until tonight."

I swirled the glass and let the light catch the dark ruby wine. I stared at it and put the day's events together in my mind. "The mayor called me to his office. Graham made a complaint about my penchant for finding dead bodies, so I promised Monty I would steer clear of any more murders." I grimaced. "Like I said to him, Dean Winters died long before I breathed on Earth, so how any of it is my fault is anyone's guess."

"I'm glad you're listening to reason and stepping away from this," Clint said. The toaster oven dinged, so he went and pulled out the piping hot pizza and put it on a plate for me. "Service with a smile. Do you want a fork?"

"No. I'm feeling bold and messy tonight. Hands only." I took a bite and a string of cheese pulled away from the top and curled onto my chin. "A napkin would be nice, though. Clearly, I haven't mastered the art of eating."

He grabbed a napkin from the holder and slid it across the table to me. "Is your visit with Monty why you went to see your mom?"

"Yes, and no. Mr. Roper also said that Mom and

137

Dean's romance was hot. Folks around here thought they would get married. She brushed it off as a teenage romance and nothing more."

Clint laughed. "Mr. Roper is the biggest gossip and an unreliable source of information. You know he claims aliens abducted him when he worked at the airport?"

I choked on my sip of wine. "What? Are you serious?"

"Oh, yeah. He claims they sucked him up into the alien ship and probed him to learn the secrets of our flying machines."

"Probed him? Yuck." I looked at my pizza, then thought of Mr. Roper and felt a little queasy.

"He hurried to reassure us it was through his nasal cavity. He felt it was important to clarify. Anyway, he wanted the Burlington police department to set up surveillance to wait for their next visitation."

I polished off my first slice. Roper probing aside, I was hungry. "I'm sure the police were thrilled. So how come you know about it?"

"When Burlington threatened to have him committed, he came to us to have us investigate Burlington Police. He believes they are colluding with the aliens." He chuckled.

"Wasn't he a baggage handler at the airport?"

"Yup, but the aliens thought he would know all about the mechanics of airplanes. How did your mom take the interrogation?"

I stuck out my hand and seesawed it. "So so. Lu will want to talk to her about Dean. It turns out that he originally planned to move to California in 1980 after he saved enough money. Suddenly, on Founder's Day, he has the means and motivation to want to hit the road the next day and wanted Mom to go with him. It's why they fought."

Clint rubbed his chin stubble. "Where'd a small-time musician come up with enough cash out of the blue to head to California? That's a cross-country trip, and even then, the cost of gas, hotels, and food would have been steep."

"That's what I thought, too." I finished the second piece of pizza and took my plate to the sink to wash it. "He had a motorcycle. I wonder what happened to it?"

"I'll text Lu this right now, so she can jump on it first thing in the morning."

I turned off the sink and faced him. "About Lu. Wait and talk to her in the morning."

Clint had his finger poised above his phone but stopped. "Why? What did you do?"

"Hey, I resent that. This was all Anthony. He bought a house and started a business in the last few days."

He leaned back in his chair and took a large sip of wine. "What?"

"That's not all. Lu must have gotten a call that the lights were on at his new place of business, and she came by tonight while I was talking to him to check it out. She knows that Anthony's here."

Clint let out a whistle. "I would love to have seen the look on her face when she saw him."

139

"I did. It wasn't pretty. She knows we didn't tell her about Anthony, and by now, she probably knows we spilled the beans about her pregnancy."

Clint poured us both another glass of wine. "I'm calling in sick tomorrow. There's no way I want to face her. Those pregnancy hormones are scary."

I considered my idea of a romantic getaway. Perhaps now was the time for us to make our escape. It wouldn't work. The library needed me, and Lu was a bloodhound. She could track us down no matter where we went. Plus, we'd eventually have to come home. "She'll be fine a year or two from now when she's forgotten all about our betrayal." I laughed. "I love Lu. She's like a burnt marshmallow. All crusty and bitter on the outside, but softness and sweetness hidden on the inside. She'll be okay. Hey. You said you had a rough day, and here I've been yammering your ear off talking about mine. What's going on?"

Clint took another big sip of wine. "Oh, it's nothing. Just my mother came back to town today."

Chapter Twenty

"What?" I screeched. "You let me yammer on about my day when you had that bomb to drop?" Now I realized why he had refilled our wineglasses on a weeknight. "How are you feeling? Are you all right? Is she staying?"

"Slow down before you hyperventilate. Let's go back to the living room. I need to relax. My whole body feels like I have knots in every muscle."

He grabbed both their glasses and the bottle of wine and went back to the living room. I hurried after him, worried. Once we settled back on the couch, I grabbed his hand. "Seriously. Are you okay? This has to be a shock. How long has it been since you've seen her?"

I had only recently learned about Clint's parents. It was a dark secret he kept to himself, and it was only when he had been shot and almost died did he tell me the entire story. Marta Mason drank and cheated on Clint's dad for years. Clint said his father was a nice guy, but weak. He ended up killing himself when Clint was a kid. His mom took off, and he ended up living in Miller's Cove with his aunt. His elderly aunt had taken care of his necessities, making sure he was clothed and fed, but she was a cold fish. Clint had spent his teenage years at our house since my brother Rick was his best friend. It's when I developed my crush on him.

"I'm fine. At least, I think I am." He picked at an invisible piece of thread on his t-shirt. "You know, I

141

played a hundred different scenarios in my head over the years. Would I hate her and curse at her the first time I saw her, or would I forgive her, and we'd reunite like you see in those stupid television dramas?"

"And?" I tightened my grip on his hand.

"And I felt nothing. I felt absolutely numb. It was as if she were a stranger who walked into the police station. Is that crazy?"

I thought about how I would feel if it were me, and I couldn't. My parents were the June and Ward Cleaver of Miller's Cove. "I don't think you can always decide how you feel. Sometimes, no matter how hard we try, our feelings just… I don't know, are. Did she say why she is here?"

Clint leaned his head back on the couch and stared up at the ceiling. He said nothing for the longest time. When he spoke, bitterness laced his words. "Not for me. No, my mom came here for nothing more than curiosity and whim. She's sober now. Has been for years, or so she said. She's got a job for some company out of Atlanta that sells medical supplies. She was driving through the area when she saw a television report identifying Dean Winters as the body found in your backyard." He looked at me. "Phee, how many times has she driven right by here and never stopped? Never called or wrote. Hell, she didn't even ask me how I was doing when she saw me."

I leaned my head on his shoulder. "I'm so sorry, Clint. That must have hurt a lot.

"It did, but it didn't." He pounded his fist on his thigh. "I don't know. Am I too broken to feel love for my mother?" He buried his head in his hands.   I wrapped my arms around him, shocked to see him like this. "Hey. You are not broken. She put you through more as a kid than most people experience in a lifetime. You can feel however you want to feel about her."

We sat there together, curled in each other's arms, lost in thought. I worried that Marta's arrival in town would hurt Clint and make him shut down his feelings again. I also wondered why Marta was so curious about Dean Winters, and why she chose now to stop in Miller's Cove.

***

I woke up the next morning on the couch. I must have fallen asleep last night when Clint and I finally stopped worrying about the appearance of his mother and distracted ourselves with an episode of the *Andy Griffith Show*. If only life was as carefree and wholesome as it was in that small town. I blinked and opened my eyes tentatively, smelling coffee. From down the hall, I could hear that Clint was already up and in the kitchen. I looked at my phone and saw it was barely past seven o'clock.

I stumbled to the bathroom and splashed cold water on my face. It did little to push the cobwebs from my sleep-deprived head. I wrapped myself in my favorite blue robe and made my way to the kitchen, yawning. I heard Clint talking to someone.

"At first I was hot enough to spit tacks," Lu said. "But it was silly of me to expect everyone to tiptoe around me."

I stopped outside in the hallway, a little apprehensive about facing Lu after last night.

"I'm just glad you came around to my way of thinking," Anthony said.

Then, what to my listening ears should I hear but the sound of Lu giggling. What a shocking, but fantastic way to start my morning after everything that happened yesterday. I hurried into the kitchen, not caring that my hair was a tangled rat's nest, and my bathrobe was older than most people.

"Good morning," I sang out.

Clint handed me a cup of coffee, raising his eyebrows at my chipper demeanor. He had already showered, shaved, and looked ready for duty, but the dark circles beneath his eyes betrayed his lack of sleep.

"What's good about it?" Lu growled. She frowned at me, but a look from Anthony and she burst into a laughter. "The look on your face was worth getting out of bed so early."

I took a tentative step towards a chair, not sure if it was safe to sit next to this chipper version of Lu. It kind of scared me if I was honest. Clint took the decision away from me when he sat down by Anthony, leaving me standing awkwardly by shifting from foot to foot.

"Sit down and enjoy your cup of coffee, Phee," Lu said. "I'm not angry with you. I was, but Anthony helped me see that everyone's been dancing around my feelings out of love. Didn't you, Baby?" She leaned into Anthony and gave him a kiss on the cheek.

Still suspicious that this was all a prank, I said, "What about keeping the baby a secret?"

Lu grimaced. "Hormones and a bad upbringing."

"What are you talking about? Your parents were wonderful last time they came to town," I said.

"Not my parents, but my high school classmates. A few girls got pregnant in high school and had to get married. You know, most of these Puerto Rican mothers will not let their daughters be single mothers. A lot of shotgun weddings my senior year. Those guys looked miserable, and the girls even more so. All but one ended in divorce after less than a year. I didn't want to be one of those women who had to get married because she got pregnant. It's the twenty-first century, for Pete's sake. Women can raise a child on their own without a man."

"But you're not a kid." I sipped my coffee and wondered if I would feel the same way if I were in Lu's shoes. Probably. A person wants to be loved for them, not for what they bring to the marriage table, like a child or money. My mind niggled away at the thought of money. *What was it?* I hadn't drunk enough caffeine to make sense of all the thoughts swirling in my head.

Anthony cleared his throat. "We have an important announcement to make."

"You're getting--"

Lu scowled. "Stop right there, Phee, and let him finish."

"As I was saying, Lu and I have decided that I will stay with her until the baby arrives. It will allow

145

me to work on the house and get it ready and launch my security business. Once we've lived together and decided if I can deal with her squeezing the toothpaste from the middle and leaving the toilet seat down, we'll discuss marriage."

I squealed. "A wedding! I have the perfect place. Well, I will if I can remove the death aura Willow claims I have."

Lu struggled to sit up, but her enormous belly made it difficult, and she sank a little lower on the kitchen chair. "We appreciate the offer, Phee, but as my Irish grandmother would say, don't put the cart before the horse."

"I don't think that's an Irish saying." Lu's growl stopped me from expounding on the origin of that idiom. "I need to get ready for work. I have a board member watching me like a dragon guards his gold, so I can't be late. Congratulations to you both. I'm thrilled you didn't shoot me last night, Lu."

"I didn't want to mess up Anthony's new floors in his office."

Although she was joking, I decided it was a good time to leave.

Chapter Twenty-One

Lu and Anthony left before I finished showering. I was over the moon that Lu hadn't shot Anthony and decided that maybe they could have a relationship. The older I got, the more I realized I had lived my life in a house of romance built on Hollywood and Harlequin lies. My love for old movies groomed me to believe that a man had to make you melt with his debonair ways. My fourteenth summer spent reading over a hundred paperback romances made me think men were all smoldering and troubled. All they needed was the love of a good woman. I also believed that women needed to be rescued by the aforementioned hot guy with no shirt and flowing blond hair. Thank goodness Juliet was my sister who broke me quickly of the idea that I needed to be rescued.

"What time will you be home tonight?" I asked Clint as I grabbed a container of leftovers for my lunch. A glance at my watch told me I didn't have time to fix anything else. I would run into Nellie's coffee shop and grab a scone and another cup of coffee on my way to the library.

Clint barely glanced up from his phone. "Don't know. I just got a text from Sheriff Dawes. Someone broke into the Lawson's home last night while they were at the church. One of the part-time deputies took a statement already, but he wants my eyes on the scene."

I hesitated before speaking, but we had left our conversation about his mother unfinished. "Should we arrange for your mother to come here to the house? I

147

mean, she's never met me, so I can make a nice dinner and we can chat."

This made him look up. "Absolutely not. I don't need her poison creeping into what I consider my haven. Leave it alone, Phee. I'm begging you to stay away from her. She's not a good person."

I didn't even argue. There were many battlefields I would pitch my tent on to argue, but I had worked too hard on making this relationship work despite his unpleasant childhood experience. I didn't need to take steps backward. I leaned down to kiss him. "Know I love you and I'm here for you."

He grabbed me and pulled me down onto his lap for a more satisfying kiss than the peck I'd given him. "I love you, too, Phee Jefferson. Please never doubt it."

A little breathless, I touched his cheek. "I won't." I wanted to crawl back into my pajamas and cuddle with him for the rest of the day, but we both had work, so I gave him a promising look and walked away.

I could have walked to Cup o' Joe and work, but the cute open-toed sandals I wore with my solid teal wrap dress weren't up to the challenge of power walking down the sidewalks of Miller's Cove. I hopped into Velma and drove the five minutes to downtown. I'd missed the early morning rush at Nellie's, so I parked my van out front and dashed in.

"I saw your van pull in. I have some fresh-baked blueberry scones. You want that and your usual coffee with two stevia and a dash of milk?" Nellie asked. She stood behind the counter with a bright blue apron emblazoned with the outline of a coffee mug and the words Nellie Jo's Cup of Joe emblazoned on the front.

"Yes, please. I like the new apron."

"It was Cincinnati's idea. He said that I need to brand myself. At first, I thought he was talking about how they do those cattle down in Texas, but then he explained that you have to have a logo and market your business." Nellie wrapped the scone in paper and placed it in a white bakery bag, then handed me my cup of coffee.

"Cincinnati's been reading too much. You're the only coffee shop in town. Who do you need to market to?" I pulled out my wallet and handed her a ten-dollar bill.

"Things are changing in Miller's Cove. The lake people want new things. They might get one of those chain coffee shops like they have off the interstate. I'm ahead of the curb," Nellie said, handing me my change.

"Curve."

"Huh?" Nellie crinkled her sharp nose, making her resemblance to a honey possum stronger than ever.

"The saying is ahead of the curve."

She waved my words away. "Whatever it is, I'm ahead. Listen. I was sitting in my living room the other night and got to thinking about that key."

"Key?" Then I realized. I had tossed the key Watson had dug from the backyard into my purse. I should have given it to Lu or Clint the moment I found it. "Yes, I still have it."

"You should drive to Burlington and have the bank verify it goes to one of their safety deposit boxes."

I picked up my cup of coffee and bakery bag. I needed to hustle if I wanted to open the library on time. "I'm going to give it to Lu. It's her case."

Nellie pulled out a rag from under the counter and wiped a nonexistent mess from the counter. She didn't meet my eyes. "That's probably best. Everyone knows you have a curse hanging over you. Look how it's followed you and caused all these problems with your sister's wedding."

"What?" I squealed. "Who said that?"

She still wouldn't meet my gaze. "Phee, you know I'm not one to gossip. I overheard someone saying you were cursed. I didn't pay them no mind and went back to work. Just thought you should know what folks are saying. The sooner they solve these murders, the sooner your curse will leave."

"I've got to get to work. Thanks for the scone." I turned on my heel and strode out the door, fuming at the idea that the town thought I was cursed. "Of all the foolish things that my sister believed in, the wedding curse tops the list."

I was so immersed in my frustration that I didn't see Juliet until I slammed into her. "Agh! Speak of the devil and she appears."

Juliet's eyes widened, and she gave me a bemused look. "Talking to yourself is a sign of early aging, Flea."

"I was muttering about you under my breath because the whole town thinks I'm cursed." I glared up at her. "And stop calling me Flea."

"Someone rolled out of the wrong side of the

bed and woke up with the grumpies."

Juliet talked to me in the same sing-song voice she used during story time yoga. Unlike the children, it didn't calm me. It made me livid. "You're going to get married and you're going to like it," I sputtered, sloshing coffee. "Just go away. I need to open the library and I'm so mad I could spit enough nails to build a barn."

I tried to stomp away, but those cute open-toed sandals made it impossible. I left with a *pop pop* sound as they slapped against the back of my foot. Cincinnati stood outside the library in his usual spot, waiting for my arrival. I paused my bull charge to change my expression. Even though Cincinnati had known me since I was born, it was important that I show my professional side when interacting with the patrons, even a friend. I didn't know who Graham had watching and reporting on my behavior. I knew it wasn't Cincinnati, but the rest of the town could watch and wag their tongues.

"Good morning," he said, easing his bulky frame from the pillar he leaned against. "What's new in the world besides the horrible performance by the Burlington Badgers? That pitcher couldn't get a ball over the base even if it was ten feet wide. Worst game I ever wasted a hot dog on."

I laughed. "Perhaps you need to pick another sport to watch."

He shook his head. "Out of the mouths of babes and gorgeous librarians. You had a mighty sour look on your face. Is that two-cent preacher giving you a hard

151

time still?"

I unlocked the door, and he followed behind me. "No. Everyone thinks I'm cursed because Dean Winters' body was buried in my backyard."

"That was a bad bit of business. Poor Craig. How he got tied up with that crowd of no-good scoundrels, I'll never know."

I put my purse on the counter and grabbed the book cart to gather things from the book drop. As was our habit, Cincinnati came with me. I was young and limber, so I squatted on the ground while he took the books and videos from my hand to line them up in Dewey order on the cart.

"I didn't think you knew them since you were older." I handed him a stack of four books. "What about my mom? I heard she and Dean dated for a while."

"He was a good-lookin' fella, but you know how you see a dog whose been kicked a few times too many and is a little too skinny?"

A vision of the commercials that aired on the weekends asking for donations to save abused and abandoned animals filled my head, along with the sad song that accompanied it. I always made Clint change the channel because they made me cry. "Yes. I have an idea on what you mean."

"Dean wanted to be a good guy. He wanted to be that person who everyone liked and was successful, but he didn't quite know how to do it."

"It makes me feel better Mom didn't date an obvious jerk." I stood up and brushed off the front of my dress. "So, what else do you remember?"

Cincinnati finished lining the books up before he answered. "That summer was a strange one. It was hotter than it had been for years, and it made people's tempers flare. The war was over, but still fresh in everyone's minds. There was another oil crisis, so everything was expensive, and people felt the pinch. Not the young people, of course. I swear I didn't think any of them had a lick of sense. The members of the band spent money on girls and flashy clothes, like their bank accounts would never see empty."

"Including my mom?"

"Your mom wasn't someone to be impressed by flashy cars, but Sheila Dawes enjoyed the fancier things. Marta Hancock was here that summer visiting her aunt. She's Clint's mama. Bunch of girls. I couldn't name them all if I could."

"So, what happened?" I asked.

He shook his head. "I couldn't tell you. After Dean left, the group fell apart. I'm guessing he was the glue that held them together. Of course, now everyone knows he didn't leave, but all of them said he left for California."

They may have all said it, but at least one of them was lying. I wish I knew which one.

Chapter Twenty-Two

I had time to check in and shelve all the returned books and run overdue reports before the first patron of the day arrived. I never counted Cincinnati since he was a fixture. Mr. Roper strolled in a half hour after I opened to return his latest western novel.

"You have another one by this author?" Mr. Roper asked.

"Not today, but one's on order. I'll put it on hold for you and call you when it's ready." I loved I could provide this close level of customer service. Whenever I longed for a job in a bigger county system, I remembered patrons would become a barcode on their card rather than a relationship. Lower pay and a smaller budget, but relationships and more autonomy balanced out the negatives.

Mr. Roper went and sat on the chair opposite Cincinnati and the two of them bickered over the minor league game the previous evening. Remembering my plan to give the key I found to Lu, I dialed the non-emergency number to the sheriff's office. I could have called Lu's cell phone, but this was official business. I may have made a kerfuffle with the photograph, but I found the key after the forensic team had searched my yard. They just hadn't torn up enough of my lawn to find it. However, I planned to do things by the book with it.

"Sheriff's office. What's going on at the library, Phee?" Tammy answered the phone. She was as much of a fixture at the sheriff's office as Sheriff Jaime

Dawes.

"How did you know it was me?" I asked.

"They did an upgrade to the phone system last week, and I have a fancy new telephone on my desk with a digital display of who is calling. Since it showed the library and you or Wade always open during the week, I figured I had a fifty-fifty chance of being right." I could hear Tammy filing her long nails through the phone. She had recently switched from plain colors to designs involving sequins and other bling. When I would go see Clint, she delighted in showing me her latest manicure.

"Is Lu in? I have something I found in my backyard that I need to give her. It may or may not relate to the Dean Winters' case."

"Sorry, Phee. She called in today. Guess that good-looking boyfriend arrived in town and she's spending some time with him. Let me patch you through to Jaime. He's in his office drinking coffee with his wife." She put me on hold and the same horrible Muzak you heard on long elevator rides filled my ears.

"Hey, Phee. What can I do for you?" Jaime's voice boomed through the phone. The sheriff epitomized large and in charge.

"Watson dug up a key in the backyard with a key ring that looks to be from the late seventies. I'm not sure if it's important or not." I pulled the key out of my purse and looked at it. It might be to a safe deposit box, but it could be for a lock or bus locker. I had no idea. It definitely wasn't like any car or house key I'd ever

155

seen.

"It's probably nothing, but I can swing by and grab it later this morning. I appreciate you calling us."

We both said the usual goodbye pleasantries and hung up. I dug around in my desk for a plain white envelope and placed the key inside it, then I wrote in clear, block letters the sheriff's name and tucked it into my top drawer. I'd let Wade know where it was just in case I was at lunch or gone for the day.

Since it was slow, I split my computer screen to show the circulation system and some of the social media marketing plans I drafted to promote some of our upcoming programs. I spent the next half hour undisturbed and finished scheduling some posts for the upcoming week. I closed out the program and saw Graham Lawson's wife had entered the library and was looking around.

She saw me staring and smiled. "Phee, right? I'm Dolores Lawson. My husband is on the board of trustees for the library."

I plastered a big, plastic smile on my face. "Yes, I met him at our last board meeting. What can I help you with, Mrs. Lawson?"

"Oh, please just call me Lola. Mrs. Lawson is my mother-in-law, and she's stuffier than a taxidermy bird in a museum. It must be where my husband learned it." She gave me a warm smile. "Graham told me what he said to you, and I came by to apologize. He sometimes buys into the image of upright, solid preacher too much and forgets that he should also remember he is a human being." Surprise must have shown on my face because she gave a quiet laugh. "Yes, I gave him my opinion that he was acting just like his mother. He didn't like that one bit. A holdover from his days in the military, I suppose."

"Thank you," I stammered. "Your nickname is Lola? You aren't, I mean weren't, Craig Muldean's stepsister, were you?"

Her smile faded. "Yes. How did you know?"

"When I discovered Craig's body, I noticed he had letters with your name on them on his table."

She motioned to the empty table near the beginning of the reference section. "Can we sit down for a minute?"

When we were seated, I leaned forward and said, "I'm sorry for your loss. My dad said you and Craig were close."

"Yes and no. We were when we were younger, but Craig hated the fact that I married Graham. I went off to college and ran into Graham when I was with some friends to a local church service. Graham was there, and when I recognized him from when I was younger, the two of us started chatting. Turns out he was an associate pastor. He had turned his life around in the military and was different."

"There were rumors that Graham was a bit of a rebel when he was younger." I thought rebel was a polite way of saying troublemaker.

She laughed. "Which was why Craig didn't like it. I tried to explain that Graham wasn't like that anymore, but he said a leopard never changes its spots."

"Had you seen Craig since you came back to

Miller's Cove?" I saw Wade come in the front door. I gave him a look that I hoped said for him to take over the circulation desk so I could finish talking to Lola."

Lola nodded. "Yes. In fact, that's probably why you saw those letters out on the table. I went to visit him the night before he died. I brought my old letters, and he pulled out some pictures. We had such a great evening talking about when our parents were married. We just reconnected and made plans for him to visit the church and meet Graham 2.0 as I like to call him. Now, he's gone, and I realize we wasted years over a silly disagreement."

"So, he and Graham hadn't talked?"

"Not in years. Graham left Miller's Cove back in the late seventies. He said he thought he'd kicked the dust off this small town. To be honest, it surprised me when he agreed to be assigned to Miller's Cove. The home office gives preachers choices for their assignments. We could have gone to Florida, but Graham said the time was right to come home."

"Does the sheriff know you're Craig's family?" I asked. I glanced at the circulation desk and saw Wade had taken over. When he saw me glance at him, he arched an eyebrow in our direction.

"Of course. Sheila called me and broke the news. I've already given my statement to that grouchy deputy. What was her name? Deputy Lucille, Lucinda… it doesn't matter. It's why Graham was out of sorts. He felt like she put me through the ringer when she questioned me." She glanced at her watch. "I need to go. Mrs. Williams had an awful night at the nursing home, and I promised her daughter that I would sit with her so Hannah can go home and change clothes."

I knew Hannah Williams and her mother. Hannah worked part time at Nellie's coffee shop because it allowed her time to stay with her mom. Mrs. Williams suffered from late-stage dementia, so Hannah valued every moment she had with her mother. I made a mental note to text her to let her know I could give her a break, too, if she needed. I said goodbye to Lola and waited until she left the library before going back to the circulation desk.

"The two of you looked like you were solving the problems of Miller's Cove and the state. Want to talk about it?" Wade asked.

"Craig Muldean was her stepbrother. She's also Graham Lawson's wife. She came to apologize for Graham's behavior."

Wade's eyes widened. "Didn't see that coming. Do you think she's sincere?"

I thought about my conversation with Lola. She seemed genuine. I still didn't like her husband, but I could like one without the other. "I do. By the way, I found an old key in the backyard that might relate to Dean Winters. The sheriff said he would stop by later to pick it up. It's in the top drawer of my desk if I'm not here."

The rest of the morning remained slow. At noon, I looked at the leftovers I'd brought for lunch and decided I'd rather take a walk downtown and window shop. I could grab a salad to bring back from the diner. I kept a pair of walking shoes in my bottom desk drawer for the days when the weather was nice or when I wore shoes that looked better in the window than they felt on my feet. I slipped them on and told Wade I'd be back.

Chapter Twenty-three

When I felt the warm sunshine on my face, I knew I'd made the right decision on those leftovers. It was gorgeous outside. I went by Anthony's office to see if he and Lu were there. Last night had been so chaotic that I hadn't toured the entire place. I was curious to see what the back looked like since it was no longer a clock repair shop.

I walked down the steps and saw Juliet leaning against Velma. She held up a piece of white fabric and waved it at me. When I ignored her and kept walking, she scurried after me. "You can't stay angry with me forever, Phee."

"I can if I want to. You're not the boss of me." I suppressed a smile. I wasn't really angry with her, just frustrated. She needed to sweat it out for a minute or two. I liked to challenge Juliet and her crazy ideas sometimes, and this was one battle I wanted to win.

"I'm your only sister, though, so you have to like me."

"That's not how that works." I stopped and turned toward her. "I'm on my way to Anthony's new office. You can tag along if you like, but I don't want to hear even a whisper about curses or anything remotely related to you and Willow's woo woo ideas."

"Anthony has an office?" Juliet's gorgeous face looked amazing even when she looked confused.

I explained to her about Anthony and Lu finding us last night and ended with Lola's visit to the library. "I want to talk to Lu and see what she learned when she talked to Lola. Make sure she's telling the truth."

Juliet had the nerve to laugh out loud and pat me on my shoulder. "That's so cute. You think you're going to interrogate Lu? Good luck. I'm coming with you so I can reassemble you when she's done tearing you to shreds."

"Her personality bordered on rainbows and unicorns this morning when she was at my house."

"But she's pregnant and some women don't handle it well. Lu's one of those women. I had a friend who actually loved being pregnant, so she's had four kids already. She says it's the only time she doesn't have PMS and migraines. But my other friend is like Lu, and it's made her irritable. Carly said it was from lack of sleep and morning sickness. She can't get comfortable, and she's been sick every morning for four months. The doctor finally gave her some medicine to help." Juliet's long legs had her in front of me in seconds.

"Slow down. I have to take two steps for each of yours. Clint's mom is back in town, too," I said.

If Juliet had brakes on her feet, she would have screeched. I ran into the back of her. "You should have told me."

She was right, of course. Clint and I had an understanding that some things would always be shared with others. Juliet was my person to share with, and Wade was his. We knew the important things would go no further than the two of them. We both thought it was important to a healthy relationship to have an outside person as a sounding board. It's one of the many things we'd discussed as we navigated our relationship. Only the bedroom was off limits as a point of discussion with Juliet. Thankfully, she'd never been one to share in that department either. We both knew women who did, and they were friends we always steered the conversation back to safer topics like the weather. Some things are sacred.

"Have you met her?" Juliet asked. "What's she like?"

I motioned for her to keep walking. "I haven't met her, and I don't think Clint wants me to. He's conflicted. He feels like he should be happy to see her, but he said he's numb."

Juliet bobbed her head. "I think I'd be the same. She chose to not be his family. It's not like she gave him up as a baby to be adopted. Instead, she dumped him on her aunt and took off."

We arrived at Anthony's new business. Today, he had the paper pulled down from the windows, and we could see him moving furniture with Lu seated behind the desk directing his efforts. We watched for a minute, amused at their body language. Lu tried to be bossy based on her expression, but Anthony kept laughing and walking over to her to kiss her. It felt good to see the two of them so happy.

I rapped on the window, and Anthony walked over and let us in the door. "Hey, you two. What's going on?"

I tried for nonchalant. "Nothing. Just on my lunch break and thought I would check to see how the office was coming."

Lu piped up from the desk. "Don't believe her. She's fishing for information about the case. I can tell by the way she's trying to hide any expression from her face. Phee, I interrogate criminals for a living. You have a horrible poker face. Please never pursue a life of crime because you will fail miserably."

I sighed. "Fine. Lola Lawson came to the library and told me she's Craig Muldean's stepsister. I wanted to make sure she was legit in her apology for her husband's behavior and that she wasn't the person who whacked poor Craig on the head."

"Do you really think she would kill her own brother?" Juliet asked.

"Stepbrother and they had a falling out over Graham years ago. And yes, everyone is a suspect until we eliminate them."

Lu gave a satisfied grunt. "Finally, you're thinking like a cop. To answer your question, she had an alibi for the time Craig died. She was with the church elders going over finances. At least ten parishioners can vouch for her whereabouts."

"Was Graham there, too?" I asked, but I knew the answer even before I asked it.

"Yes. The construction of the church is over budget, so he called a meeting to discuss it." Lu shifted, then gave a small grimace. "Junior is playing soccer on my bladder."

Juliet zeroed in right away. "Junior? So, the baby is a boy?"

Anthony chuckled. "She hasn't told me, so I doubt she'll tell you."

"Lu, Junior. I'm waiting until he or she is born. The world puts too many expectations on a baby before they are even born. Will they look like the father? Are they smart like their Aunt Jean? Will they have their weird cousin Alvin's love of broccoli on ice cream?" Lu settled back in her seat and rubbed her belly. "Baby will be whoever they want to be."

"Who eats broccoli on ice cream?" I asked and gagged. "Some people shouldn't ever go in a kitchen."

"My weird cousin Alvin," Lu said. "We hated summers at the ice cream truck with him. He thinks it counterbalances all the fat and sugar in the ice cream. He's a killjoy on about fifty other things, too."

"I need to get back to work soon, and I haven't grabbed a bite to eat yet. Before I leave, can I look at the back room, Anthony? Does it still look like a clock repair workshop? I have an image of Victorian England and a character from Dickens working away in the back," I said.

"I hate to disappoint you, but I tore all the shelves and the workbench down. I want to make room for my future staff, and I'll install state-of-the-art equipment. You're welcome to look."

I skirted around the furniture still not in place and walked to the back room. Anthony was right. It was a huge letdown. I could see his vision for the space, though. In the back was an exit to the rear of the building, a door marked as a bathroom, and a rickety set of stairs. I walked back to the front. "Where do the stairs go?"

"An old storage space in the attic filled with

junk. I'm going to tear down those stairs next week and put up a proper set of steps with a handrail."

"You're very handy," Juliet said. "I'll keep you in mind when I do a studio remodel."

Lu patted Anthony and said, "This handyman is mine, ladies. Get your own."

"I come from a long line of men who are handy around the house. I can do repairs, build small structures, paint a fence. Besides, if I don't know how to do it, there's probably a video online walking you through step-by-step."

Juliet and I said goodbye and wished them luck with their furniture arrangement. We were halfway up the street before I spoke. "That struck my prime suspect and current arch nemesis off my list."

"You have an arch nemesis?"

"Graham Lawson. He made the perfect criminal. Smarmy. Self-important. Fleecing his flock of their hard-earned money. To be honest, I'd mentally pinned everything on him. Now, I need to start all over again."

"Have you struck Mom off the list?"

"Yes, but only because it's Mom. Not because I have any evidence that clears her."

"Let's meet up tonight at my place. I'll call Willow and between the three of us, we'll look at all the evidence."

"Should we ask Lu? She's always been part of our group," I said.

"I suppose, but I think she's probably too wrapped up in her reunion with Anthony to have time for us."

My phone buzzed. I glanced down and saw a message from Wade saying that the envelope with the key had been picked up and could I grab him a sandwich from the diner, too.

I was quiet all the way to the diner. Glancing around at the tables full of the residents of Miller's Cove, I wondered if any of them were the murderer. It was a chilling thought, and as soon as the food was ready, I grabbed the bag and darted out the door.

Chapter Twenty-four

The rest of the workday passed blissfully quiet and free from drama. It was a beautiful spring day, so most people spent their afternoon outside rather than inside the library. When our part-time circulation clerk arrived after the high school let out, I saved my documents and shut down my office computer.

When I arrived home, I changed into a pair of faded blue jeans with non-fashion holes in the knees and an old t-shirt. After feeding Ferdie and the dogs, I took them out back with me to play while I weeded the flowerbeds.

"Hello, Phee." Mrs. Lancaster called over our shared white fence.

My face grew hot as I remembered my promise to visit several days ago. "Mrs. Lancaster, I'm so sorry I forgot to come see you. It's no excuse, but with the dead body and Juliet not wanting to get married…"

She opened the gate and came into my backyard. "Pshaw. Don't worry about it. I'm sure Graham cornering you in the library after our board meeting didn't help."

"You overheard?"

She sat down on one of my wrought iron garden chairs. "I made a point of standing outside the door. I hope you don't mind."

"Of course not." I pulled off my work gloves and sat opposite her. "Do you think I'm a liability to the library?"

"If I did, you would know it. Phee, I've never

168

been one to couch my words in flowers and feel-goods."

I knew what she said to be true, which is why I quivered in my slippers that I forgot to come visit her. Mrs. Lancaster was the unofficial matriarch of Miller's Cove and the president of the library's board of trustees. "I really don't try to find dead people. I only wanted to build a gazebo so my baby sister could get married and now, it's a big mess and —" To my utter dismay, I burst into tears. "Everything's a mess. Juliet thinks her wedding is cursed. Willow says it's my bad karma. Mom used to date the dead guy. And sweet Mr. Muldean is dead. How did everything get to be so hard?"

Mrs. Lancaster, to her credit, didn't get up and go back to her house. I wouldn't have blamed her if she had. Instead, she sat quietly and let me wail about my problems before speaking. "You're not cursed, and your sister has strange ideas. Everyone knows it, but it's what makes her unique. She has the gentlest heart. I've seen her with some of our less able friends down at the senior center. She is so patient and kind. We can all give her a little grace with her eccentricities."

I sniffled. "You're right. She is fantastic with people."

"As for sweet Mr. Muldean, it's why I wanted to talk to you. He wasn't always a sweet, old man who gave children lollipops. I used to teach him in Sunday school when he was a child, and a person knows when someone isn't right."

"What do you mean?" I wiped my eyes.

"He had a cruel streak. If you crossed him when he was a child, he would watch and wait until you didn't expect it, then trip you or kick your chair from beneath you. It wasn't just other kids. He did it to adults, too. Horrible child."

"But he outgrew it, right?"

She nodded. "I suppose. Either that or he just changed his ways. Through the years, I've heard rumors he wasn't above a little blackmail. Nothing prosecutable, of course. For example, Monty had a small indiscretion with a woman in Burlington. Somehow, Craig learned about it and lo-and-behold, Monty pushed through Craig's permit to expand his hardware store even though it wouldn't comply with code."

"Did people find out about Monty?"

She shook her head. "No, and please keep that tidbit to yourself. I know because I demanded a meeting with Monty, and he confessed his sins. He knows I'm a vault."

This shed new light on who could have killed Mr. Muldean and Dean. I hadn't truly considered Monty a suspect, even though I knew he was one of the group so many years ago. "What about the band The Screaming Goats?"

"A bunch of screaming hooligans is more like it. All loud guitars and crashing cymbals." Mrs. Lancaster clucked her tongue. "Sam LeVere was the only one with a decent moral compass. He would play with the band, but most of the time he worked on the family dairy farm. Such a shame."

I knew Sam LeVere couldn't have killed Craig, so he was struck off the suspect lift for Dean, too. The cases had to be related and now with the blackmail thrown into the mix, it started to gel in my mind. "My mom and Sheila used to hang out with the guys in the band. Mom dated Dean."

"Your mother is a good woman. Dean Winters was her one slip in judgment. I could see Sheila dating him. She liked the bad boys when she was a teenager."

I laughed. "I doubt the sheriff would be considered a bad boy."

"No, he's an honest man. I think leaving here and going to school helped her grow up. Her dad used to do work for me. Landscaping and he built my patio back. She used to come and help him sometimes. Sheila might have been wild, but her dad was her world. He passed away not too long after she graduated from college. He used to brag about her when he would come mow my lawn. Her mom died when Sheila was twelve. Cancer."

Poor Sheila. Once again, I felt relieved that I had such wonderful parents who were still with me. "What about Graham Lawson?"

She picked up a glove to wave a pesky fly that landed on the table. "Graham is a study in contrasts. Good family, but he was a cocksure young man who thought he knew everything, and the world owed him more than what he already had. Graham's a taker which is why I'm surprised her volunteered to serve on the library board."

"Libraries improve everyone's image," I said.

171

"True. It makes him look good to his parishioners. I'm not a fan of the way he runs his church finances, but I heard rumors that he's up to his neck in debt with the home he and Lola built."

"Do you think he's dipping his fingers into the virtual collection plate?"

She shook her head. "No. I have a friend who is one of the church elders. Their accounting is very transparent, but if he is able to increase the parishioners and the money, then the elders might see their way to increasing his salary."

I never thought about preachers needing money and raises, but they were human, too. I had been naive to think they didn't ever think about the material things in life. "Cincinnati told me Graham was in the military."

"He was." She tapped her neatly manicured fingertip on the table. "There were rumors at the time that he got caught stealing a car in Burlington. Joyriding. His family got him out of it, of course, but his dad gave him the choice between joining the military or getting kicked out."

"Does his family live around here? I don't recall any Lawsons."

"No. They moved back in 1983." Mrs. Lancaster stood and slipped her gloves on. "I need to go finish watering my plants. It was good seeing you, dear. Tell Clint I said hello."

"I will." After she left, I pulled out my phone and called Clint. It went straight to his voicemail. He must be busy. I would see him this evening and tell him about Craig and his blackmail scheme. A few minutes later I received a text from him.

My mother showed up at the station. I'll be late tonight, so don't wait up. Love you.

Cryptic and worrying. I hoped Marta wouldn't cause Clint any grief. I wanted to talk to him, but I swallowed my need to know everything right then. I had to trust he would be fine. I returned to my flower bed and tugged at a persistent patch of wire grass that had taken root. As I pulled at the grass, I pulled at the thread of a thought. In movies and books, murders usually happened because of money, love, or revenge. If I figured out the motive for Dean's murder, it would lead to the motive for Craig's. If only I could unravel the clues.

Chapter Twenty-five

When I arrived at Juliet's that night, I was surprised to see Lu's car parked in front. I hoped she and Anthony hadn't already had a falling out. I climbed the outside stairs to her apartment. She had an inside set of stairs from the yoga studio as well, but it was after hours, and the studio was dark. Wade navigated the stairs well with his prosthetic leg, but when he was confined to the wheelchair at times, he had to hoist himself up the stairs with his arms with Juliet following closely behind him to make sure he didn't fall. It made me shudder with fear for him every time I watched. The two of them had started to look for a one-story house nearby and planned to rent the upstairs out to a young couple for extra income. If she canceled the wedding, would Juliet cancel buying a house with Wade?

I gave a determined knock on her door. I would figure this crime out or my years of reading Nancy Drew and Agatha Christie were pages down the toilet.

Wade opened the door. He had a light jacket slung over one arm. "Hello and goodbye. I'm off to help Anthony paint. I decided to leave you fine women to hash over things without me. They're in the kitchen."

I found Willow, Izzy, Lu, and Juliet seated around her enormous wooden farm table. I'm still amazed she was able to convince a group of high school football players to haul it up the steps. The thing must weigh a few hundred pounds, and it seated eight people with elbow rood. When I had asked her why she needed such a large table, she said it was, so she had room to create. It served as desk, dining table, creative space, and anything else she needed.

Juliet handed me a glass of cabernet. "Let the crime-solving begin."

Lu looked at her glass of water with sad eyes. "When this baby is born, I'm going to drink a beer."

"I have heard it's good for milk production," Willow said. "I have some information from a friend of mine who is part of the brea—"

Izzy covered her ears. "La la la. Teenager in the room who is freaked out about conversations on babies, boobs, or birth."

"Agree one hundred percent with you, there, kid," Lu said. "I'm here under duress. When Juliet called, I knew I needed to come to keep you two out of trouble." She looked at Juliet and me and pointed a finger at us.

"Us? We have no intention of doing anything stupid tonight," Juliet said. "I still have nightmares of being an appetizer for a gator. My days of breaking into buildings is over."

Lu harrumphed but let it go. "Let me lay out the ground rules. I will not discuss critical case information. Don't even ask me. I will ask you questions if you reveal anything new. I won't condone any breaking into funeral homes, pickle factories, or banks. Is everyone clear?"

"Crystal," Willow said.

"Yeah, yeah," Juliet chimed in.

I nodded and Izzy's eye just grew wide. She was in awe of Lu, I could tell.

Juliet placed a giant fuchsia sticky note on the table. "I found these handy when I taught new sequences to the senior citizens. Super-sized and cheerful." She handed each of us a black marker. "I thought this could be our murder board. I don't have a dry erase board, so this will have to do."

"I think we need to write the victims' names in the center." I said. I leaned down and wrote in my best schoolgirl penmanship Dean and Craig and drew a line. In smaller print, I wrote The Screaming Goats. "These two were connected in 1979 by their band, The Screaming Goats."

Juliet added a circle and wrote Graham inside it. I added Mom. Juliet shot me an evil glare and on the other side of Dean's name she made a larger circle and wrote Monty. I wrote Sheila's name. We stepped back. The victims' names were in the center with a circle of suspects surrounding them.

"You forgot the last guy in the band. What was his name?" Willow asked. She stood poised to write it.

"Sam LaVere, but he's dead," I said.

Lu munched on a carrot stick. "You have to add him. The first mistake you're all making is to assume one person committed both crimes. Until you've eliminated all the other suspects, you could still be looking at two murderers."

"What are the odds of that?" Izzy asked. She had been transfixed by her phone, but we must be more interesting than whatever doom scrolling she'd been doing.

"I don't know, but it's sloppy detective work to

eliminate a possibility at the beginning of an investigation," Lu said. "Juliet, can you bring me some more dip. Baby's hungry."

Juliet went to her fridge and pulled out a glass dish with her homemade ranch dip. I don't know what she put in it, but it was amazing. I begged her for the recipe all the time, but she would smile and say it was a family secret.

"Okay. We can eliminate him for Craig's death, but not for Dean's." I made an X next to his name with a C. "Graham Lawson and his wife were accounted for during Craig's death as well. They had a meeting with the church elders. Lola is Craig's stepsister, but they were estranged. According to her, the two of them visited the night before his death to try to make peace and ended up looking at old pictures and letters."

"Which is how you found the picture of Mom and Dean," Juliet chimed in.

I glared at her. Why would she remind Lu of my crime scene tampering? "Moving on. It still leaves us with Sheila, Monty, and Mom for Craig's death."

Willow shook her head. "Your mom's safe for Craig's death. I called her that morning to discuss Juliet's wedding and your bad aura, Phee."

"She could have been anywhere. That's why they're mobile phones," Izzy glanced up from her phone.

"I called her land line. You know how I feel about cell towers. They send bad electrical signals to your brain. I keep telling you that every day you talk on that thing, you're losing brain cells," Willow said to

Izzy.

Izzy held up her phone. "I don't talk. I text. My brain is huge. I can afford to lose one or two cells."

Juliet hid a smile by sipping her wine. "That leaves Monty and Sheila."

"Juliet, I asked you to talk to Sheila. Did she say anything that would tie her to Craig or Dean?" I asked.

She looked up at the ceiling then down at her feet. "I didn't get a chance. Before you read me the riot act, she didn't show up to my Reiki class. I called her to make sure she was okay, but she was really short. She said she was fine and decided Reiki wasn't her thing. It hurt my feelings, to be honest."

Lu looked at our makeshift murder board. "What are their motives? Why would either of them kill Dean and/or Craig? It's why this case is freezing rather than heating up."

"I can help with Monty's motive for Craig. I don't know about Dean," I said. I related everything Mrs. Lancaster had told me about Craig and his mini blackmail scheme.

"Interesting," Lu said, rubbing her belly. For all we know, Craig could have been blackmailing any or all of them. When we pulled his finances, his hardware store was paid for, no mortgage, and an extremely healthy bank account."

"Who wants to interrogate Sheila?" I asked.

Juliet touched her nose and called, "Not it."

"Well-played, Juls, but if I have to do it, you're coming with me." I turned to Lu. "Did you find anything out about the key I found or was that a dead end?"

Lu looked confused. "What key?"

I met her confused look with one of my own. "Watson dug a key out of the backyard near where Dean's body was buried. I put it in an envelope and called the sheriff's office. Wade said it had been picked up."

"Not by me and I saw the sheriff right before I left work. He didn't say anything about it. Hold on. Let me call him." Lu pulled out her phone and tapped the screen. "Sheriff, it's Lu. Did you find out anything about the key Phee Jefferson found at her place?"

We all stood silently watching, straining to hear. Although Jaime Dawes's voice usually boomed, I couldn't hear his response. Lu nodded her head. "I see. Got busy and forgot about it. No problem. You have a good evening, sir." She disconnected and laid the phone down on the table. "He didn't pick it up."

"I'm calling Wade." Juliet pulled out her own phone and placed it on speaker. When Wade picked up, she said, "Hey, babe. Gotcha on speaker so no sexy talk."

"Anthony was looking forward to listening in on that one," Wade's deep voice echoed through Juliet's kitchen.

I leaned forward. "You said the envelope in my top drawer got picked up. Who came by the library to get it?"

"The sheriff's wife," Wade said. "She told me that the sheriff got stuck on a conference call with another county and asked her if she would run by and

179

get it. Why?"

"We're not sure. Thanks. I'll see you when you get home," Juliet said.

Lu pushed back from the table and struggled to stand. "No way. The sheriff would never have someone pick it up. It would destroy the chain of evidence. I need to talk to Clint. If the sheriff is a part of this and doing a cover-up..." Her voice trailed away as she considered the possibilities.

"Jaime didn't even live here when Dean was killed," I said. "There's no way he's involved in this. He's my dad's best friend."

"That leaves us with Sheila," Willow said, her face grim.

We stared at the table with the names of our victims and our suspects. In my mind, I saw a red bullseye smack dab on Sheila's name.

Juliet broke the silence first. "She was Mom's best friend in high school."

I pulled at that small thread of a clue. "But Mom said Sheila and Dean had more in common and were always talking. There's something else to. Mom said that Dean planned to leave for California in 1980, but all of a sudden, he had enough cash to get out of town and wanted her to come with him. The two of them fought and she went home."

"Do you think Sheila overheard Dean asking Mom to leave that night?" Juliet asked. "Would she really kill him over a teenage crush?"

Willow and Izzy looked back and forth from Juliet and I trying to track our conversation. Lu stayed silent, lost in her own thoughts. I picked up a chip and dipped it, munching as I started to pull it all together. I thought about the band and the people in the town, and like a bolt of lightning striking me, I had an idea. "People murder other people for money, love, or revenge. What if Lu was right and two different people committed the crimes?"

Lu threw her hands up in the air. "Finally, she listens to me."

I sat down at the table and picked up the marker. "Just listen. I think that The Screaming Goats were robbing banks back in the seventies."

"What kind of shenanigans is flitting through your brain?" Juliet scoffed.

"You mock, but I did some research and that year, two local banks were robbed. I think it was Craig, Dean, Graham, and possibly Sam LeVere, but I don't think so. Three men robbed the banks. They had to have a getaway driver. I think that person was Sheila. She lost her scholarship and needed money. Graham was a greedy person according to the people who knew him. Craig's business and home were paid for. Dean had enough money to leave for California."

"It's a working theory, but can you prove it?" Lu crossed her arms, then uncrossed them. "This baby is more active than a monkey on a jungle gym."

"I don't know if I can prove it, but you might be able to get a confession. What's the statute of limitations on bank robbery in this state?" I asked.

"Oh! I know this one," Izzy piped in. "I learned about it when we were studying crime and punishment in our civics class. One of the kids did a presentation and said that there is no statute for murder by five years for bank robbery."

"The kid's right," Lu said. "That's in both the federal and state."

"So, if Graham was one of these robbers, the statute of limitations has run. He can tell us if Sheila was part of the gang," Juliet said, slowly. "Clever, Flea."

"I know. And stop calling me Flea."

"There's no statute on murder," Lu said. "If Graham killed Dean, then he's not going to spill his guts over any of this."

"It's a gamble, and today I'm feeling lucky. I think Craig Muldean killed Dean and took the money. He laid low for years with the cash. Graham left to go in the military. Sheila left for community college. Sam was busy on the farm. No one was around to notice if he had more money than usual. I think he was careful, and he groomed the face he showed the public. Sweet Mr. Muldean, but he still had a touch of evil and when the chance came up for him to blackmail Monty, he couldn't resist. It's probably the only time his mask slipped."

"That's fine, but where does Sheila come into all of this?" Willow asked.

"I think Sheila believed for all these years that Dean had taken the money and run off to California. When we found his body, she realized that he never left, and someone had killed him. She probably planned to talk to each of them, but Craig was first on her list.

He probably told her she was out of luck. Remember, she lost her chance to go to university and could only afford community college. It changed the entire trajectory of her life. Money from the robberies would have allowed her to leave the state and have something different."

Lu stood up. "It's a solid theory, but it's just that. A theory. Listen, I need to go home. Have Clint call me the minute you see him." She waddled to the door. I watched her as she grabbed her belly again and rubbed it.

"Wait up, Lu," I said. "I'll walk with you. Clint's busy with some personal stuff, but I think I need to be home when he gets there." I looked back at the rest of the women. "We'll talk about it some more tomorrow. We just need to get the evidence and you'll see I'm right."

"We? Who is this we?" Lu grumbled as she waddled down the steps. "The only we in this investigation is me and this baby."

Chapter Twenty-six

"Do you want me to drive you home?" I asked Lu. She really did look miserable.

"No. Just walk with me to Anthony's new place. It's only a few blocks from here." She chuckled. "I can't believe he gave up his career for me. Crazy."

"Why not? He loves you. And he's so excited for this baby."

She slowed her walk. "I should be livid that you spilled the beans, but the fact that he was already here to win me back. It's telling me that he wants to be with me for me, not the butter bean in my belly."

"You will be awesome parents. I'm happy the two of you are together." I looked at her face as she grimaced again. "Are you all right?"

She sat down on one of the benches the town had placed strategically around downtown. "I need to rest a minute. The baby is really active, and I keep having pains from him moving his feet against my ribs. It feels like I have a belt around my waist."

I could feel the blood drain from my face. "Are you sure you aren't in labor?"

"Definitely. I still have a month to go. There are these things called Braxton Hicks contractions. It's like warming up for the big performance. They are perfectly normal."

I sat down next to her on the bench. "That key Sheila picked up. I think she was looking for the money that they stole. Maybe she thought Dean hid it there."

"Possibly, but I think you were right when you

said Craig took the cash from Dean when he killed him. It makes sense now that we know about how flush with cash he's been over the years. If you were careful, you could live well for years. Robbers get caught because they flash the cash too much. Craig was not a stupid man."

A car turned down the street, and its headlights temporarily blinded me. When the stars cleared from my vision, I saw it was the sheriff's SUV. I waved at him, hoping he would help me convince Lu to accept a ride to Anthony's house. The SUV slowed and the window went down. Sheila Dawes was behind the wheel. "Are you two okay? Need any help?"

Startled, I blurted out, "Wade said you picked up the key I left for Jaime." As soon as the words left my mouth, I wanted to reel them back in.

"Be quiet," Lu hissed. "We're fine, Mrs. Dawes. Just sitting her chatting about the baby. Tell your husband I'll see him bright and early in the morning."

She smiled, but it didn't reach her eyes. "I will. Any progress on Craig's murder, Lu. You know Jaime. Always keeps things to himself. Craig was an old friend. Phee, he was friends with your mom, too."

"She told me," I said, matching her cold smile with one of my own.

"Nothing yet, Mrs. Dawes. Hoping it won't go cold, but you never know. New evidence might come to light. Need to put the old nose to the grindstone and question some more people," Lu said. "You have a good evening, Mrs. Dawes."

"If you're sure there isn't anything I can do to

help you… good night." Sheila closed the window and put the SUV back into drive. She pulled slowly away from the curb.

"Whew. That was close," I said, standing and holding my hand out to Lu to help her.

"You almost blew it. You really should stick to books and movies. Suspect interrogation isn't your strength. Thanks." She grabbed my hand, and I almost crumpled to my knees as she tightened her grip. "Sorry. Another Braxton Hicks contraction."

We walked up the street and were next to Anthony's new security business when I heard the squeal of tires. A quick glance behind us, and I saw the SUV barreling down the street. It jumped the curb and headed straight at us. I shoved Lu into the alley and felt the heat of the engine as Sheila screeched past us. A moment later, I heard it stop. I dared a peek around the brick wall and saw her creeping down the road back toward us.

"Help me," Lu whispered. "I've got a key to the back door. We can get inside and call for help."

I wrapped my arm around her waist and the two of us ran like ducks after a bug to the back of the building. Lu pulled a key ring from her pocket and whispered, "Glad Anthony insisted I take the keys this morning. He said it was a demonstration of his trust in me."

"His trust might save our lives." I snatched the keys from her as she gasped and grabbed her stomach again.

"Oh, no." Lu looked down at her feet.

186

"What?" I hissed, as I helped her inside.

"My water broke. That's not supposed to happen. I still have three weeks and—" She didn't finish her sentence. "Get me to that chair."

I helped her to the chair and then hurried back to the door to lock it behind us. I pulled out my phone and dialed Anthony.

He answered on the first ring. "What's up, Phee?"

"Lu's in labor," I whispered. "And the sheriff's wife is trying to kill us."

"What? Say it again. The sheriff's wife tried to kill you?"

"Yes," I hissed. "Call Clint. Call the ambulance. Call the cavalry. Just get someone to us, now!"

"Where are you? Wade, Lu's in labor." I heard the jingle of keys and a door slamming behind him. "Wade and I are on the way. Where arc you?"

"Hiding out in your office. Anthony, Sheila tried to run us over. She's the one that killed Craig Muldean. You need to get in touch with Clint. But hurry." I glanced at Lu who was gritting her teeth through another contraction.

"Stay on the line, Phee. I'm on my way. Tell Lu I'm coming."

I dropped the phone on the desk by Lu and knelt in front of her. "Are you okay?"

"No. Phee, the baby is coming now. I don't think I'm going to make it to the hospital. It's too soon."

"Baby's come out a few weeks early and are

perfectly fine. Anthony's on his way, and they're calling Clint." I started to pant.

Lu glared at me. "What are you doing?"

"Doing the breathing thing I see in the movies. It will help you get through the pain." I demonstrated again. Headlights glinted through the front windows of the office, and Lu instinctively tried to duck.

"Ouch. Phee, I'm having this baby right now." She shifted her body from the chair onto the ground. "There's a bunch of clean work rags next to the bathroom. Go grab them."

"But--"

"Now, Phee." She gritted her teeth.

I scurried across the floor, keeping low, and found the unopened bag of white cloths. I ripped them open and grabbed a handful. I rushed back to Lu. "What do I do next? Can you keep the baby in until the ambulance or Anthony or anybody but me is here to help you?"

Lu emitted a wail that she quickly suppressed. Through teeth that looked ready to crack under the strain, she said, "Reach into my pocket. I've got a pen knife and a mini flashlight attached to my house keys."

"I can't cut this baby out of you, Lu. I just can't." My hands shook as I reached and found the keys with the knife attached.

"I don't need you to cut the baby out. Cut my pants. I'm in too much pain to take them off. I can feel this baby, Phee. Do it. And do it now."

With hands that shook more than a Florida native in an Alaska winter, I carefully sliced her pants, praying I wouldn't nick her skin. Once that was done, she laid back down and said, "I'm going to push this baby out, Phee. I've done all the training. Cops know how to do this in an emergency, and this is an emergency. I'm counting on you. You're my best friend."

I was her best friend. The words gave me courage. "Tell me what to do."

So as the sound of sirens filled the air outside, Lu's wails of pain filled the dark lit only by the tiny flashlight on the ground. Moments later, I used a cloth to gently clean the little girl's face as she entered the world, crying and angry, just like her mama.

The front door to the office blew open as Anthony and Wade rushed in. Wade did an immediate spin and turned away. "Baby alert. I'll step outside and let the ambulance know where to go."

"Can I introduce you to your daughter, Anthony?" I laid the baby gently into Lu's arms. Her face was damp with perspiration, but it was the happiest I'd ever seen her.

"A daughter," Anthony said, eyes wide with awe. "I'm a dad."

"You're a dad," Lu whispered and looked down at their baby. "Angelica Rose, for each of our grandmothers."

"You remembered," Anthony's eyes filled with tears. "I love you, Lu."

"I love you, too, Anthony. And our baby girl."

I stood up and walked away to give them some

189

privacy. The sound of a stretcher being wheeled through the front and Clint's voice, made me realize that Sheila must be gone. I ran to the front to find Wade stopping Clint at the door.

"Phee," Clint pushed past Wade. "He told me you were okay, but I needed to see for myself. How's Lu?"

"Lu's fine and the proud mama bear to a little girl cub named Angelica Rose."

He pulled me into his arms. "I'm glad you're not hurt. Wade said something about Sheila Dawes trying to kill you. What in the world is he talking about?"

I buried my face against his chest, then said, "It's a long story, and you're going to want to have a seat for this one."

Chapter Twenty-seven

"The wedding was simply lovely, dear," Mrs. Lancaster said. She looked around at my garden. "You did an amazing job with the flowers, too. I wish my yard looked half this good."

"I had a little help from Senator Campbell." I glanced across the yard to where the senator stood talking about the world's problems with my parents. "He wanted Anthony to have a spectacular wedding at someplace fancy, but Lu wanted it simple with friends and family."

"It was a beautiful ceremony. Reverend Taylor always does such a nice job."

"He does. It was a feat to pull all of this together so quickly. If not for Senator Campbell, who knows where the ceremony might have been."

Willow and Izzy wandered over to us. After chatting politely for a few minutes, Mrs. Lancaster excused herself to talk to Monty. He still looked shell-shocked over everything that had gone on with his old friends.

The state police had tracked Sheila Dawes to the airport in Burlington where they arrested her for an initial charge of assault with a deadly weapon. The weapon being her car. She quickly caved and admitted she killed Craig Muldean in a fit of anger when he told her that he had killed Dean all those years ago and taken the money after he found out Dean planned to take all of the loot and run off to California. She also admitted to driving the getaway car for Graham, Dean, and Craig for the two bank robberies. She claimed she had been desperate after losing her scholarship and needed her chance to get out of the state and start life over again. No charges were brought for the robberies since the statute of limitations ended thirty-five years before, but she was now facing second-degree murder charges. The key I found in the backyard didn't have anything to do with the case. Sheila had taken it on the off chance it could tie her to the robberies, Dean, or Craig. The fear of being caught had made her paranoid.

Jaime Dawes had stepped down as sheriff immediately and Clint was acting sheriff until the election in the fall. Sheila said he knew nothing about her past, but the taint would always be there. He had put their house up for sale and left to stay with my uncle at his remote cabin. He said he would stand by his wife, but we knew her crime had broken him.

Graham denied any wrongdoing, but the home office for his church reassigned him to a small town in the middle of the Nevada desert. He left without Lola. She decided that she wanted to stay in Miller's Cove. She still didn't believe that her stepbrother who had always been so protective of her turned out to be such a louse. It would take time, but it didn't matter. Craig Muldean wasn't the person we all thought him to be, but he was still the kindly gentleman who gave me a lollipop when I visited his store.

"Penny for your thoughts, Flea," Juliet nudged me with her bare foot.

I looked down and sighed. "I can't believe you got married in your bare feet."

"I can't believe I got Lu to get married in her bare feet," Juliet shot back. "I wanted to feel closer to Mother Nature. Thank you, Flea. The wedding — both weddings — were beautiful. It was unique."

"Angelica slept through the whole ceremony."

"She's probably afraid to cry. Lu's a force to be reckoned with," Juliet said. "She is the sweetest baby."

"Makes you long for one of your own?" I asked, cocking an eyebrow.

"Not anytime soon. I'm a great auntie. Where's Clint?"

I gave a subtle nod to the porch where Clint sat with his mother. "He's trying to have a relationship with Marta. Turns out, she heard about Dean's body being found and the news mentioned Clint by name, so it sparked some small bit of maternal instinct in her. I don't know if they'll ever have a good relationship, but who knows? Stranger things have happened. She's leaving tomorrow, so we'll see if she keeps in touch."

Juliet leaned over and hugged me. "Getting married to Wade is the best thing I've ever done. The goddess approves."

"My so-called curse is gone?"

Willow chimed in and said, "My spirit guides told me that there might be another wedding at this house in the near future."

I met Clint's gaze and raised my glass to Willow's spirit guides. "Bring it on. I'm ready," I whispered.

AMY E. LILLY

The End

Bonus material
Available exclusively on Kindle Vella

Death Kicked the Milk Bucket

Chapter One

Claire stomped out of the building. Her attempt to slam the door failed miserably. It eased shut and closed with a soft whoosh of air. The large, overstuffed tote bag filled with ten years of her career slipped off her shoulder. She struggled to carry it all to her old Volvo parked in the company parking lot. As she yanked the tote bag back up, the strap ripped, and everything tumbled to the pavement.

"Dang it! If one more bad thing happens, I swear I won't be responsible for my actions!" Claire yelled to the empty lot. With a sigh, she bent down to gather up her belongings and heard a tearing sound as her pencil skirt split down the back. "Really? You have got to be kidding me. I guess that's what I get for challenging the universe." She finished gathering up her files and desk knickknacks and stuffed them back into her tote. Fumbling around in her purse to find her keys, she gave a triumphant "ha" when she yanked them free.

195

As she popped open the trunk, Claire heard a tiny mew coming from the dumpster. She slammed the trunk shut. Another small meow. She walked to the dumpster and peered inside. Nestled in a small cardboard box surrounded by garbage and rotting food was a tiny orange kitten. It looked up at her with sea green eyes and let out another meow.

"Poor little thing. Are you hungry? Somebody must have dumped you here and left you to fend for yourself. Probably someone like Jonathan Grimes, world's most horrible boss. Excuse me. Former box." Claire reached into the dumpster, lifted the fluffy orange kitten, and snuggled it to her chest. The kitten let out a contented purr and kneaded its tiny paws against her. "Well, you and I are just having a bad day. I got thrown out like trash, too. Would you like to come home with me?" As if it understood her, the kitten meowed and purred louder. Laughing, Claire picked carried it to her car. She pulled a t-shirt from her gym bag, settled the furry bundle onto the passenger seat, then headed for her apartment.

When she arrived home, Claire poured a small bowl of milk for the kitten. "I guess you need a name. How about Gingersnap?" She sat down on the kitchen floor and stroked the kitten's back. "You can be Ginger for short." The buzz of her cellphone interrupted her. She struggled up from the floor to answer.

"Hey, lady. How was your day?" Isabella asked. In the background, Claire heard the children laughing and yelling. "Knock it off you little monsters! I'm trying to talk, and I can't hear over your screeching."

After years of friendship, Claire was used to Isabella carrying on multiple conversations while on the phone.

"I got fired," Claire said. She picked at the edges of her fingernail polish, a nervous habit that ruined more than one expensive manicure.

"Oh my gosh. What happened?" Isabella asked. "Please be quiet. Go play in your room until dinner's ready. Matthew quit hitting your brother. Sorry, Claire. They're out of control with their dad out of town this week. Tell me everything."

"Nothing happened. Mr. Grimes called me into his office and went on and on about the economic downturn and how sacrifices needed to be made...blah blah blah. Five minutes later, I am in HR signing papers. Before the ink was dry, a security guard told me I had one hour to pack my desk and leave the building. Ten years on the job and I'm kicked to the curb like two-day old fish. It wasn't just me. There were two other people let go today." Claire slumped onto her overstuffed couch, kicked off her heels, and put her feet up on the coffee table.

"I am so sorry. What are you going to do?" Isabella asked.

"No clue, but I don't even want to think about it tonight. I'll worry about it tomorrow. Darrin is supposed to take me out tonight. He called this morning and said he needed to see me. Maybe he'll finally pop the question. He's been very secretive lately. I'm pretty sure he's been ring shopping. I'll be Mrs. Stanislowski. Wife of Dr. Stanislowski. Claire Stanislowski." Claire let the name roll off her lips. "It sounds kind of posh."

"If you say so." She was not a fan of Darrin. In her opinion, he was boring and uptight. "I've got to get dinner ready before the kids eat the dog. Text me when you get home tonight."

"Will do." Claire disconnected and pulled herself up from the couch. Darrin would be there to pick her up soon, so she needed to hurry and get ready. He hated to be kept waiting. She pulled off her now ruined skirt and kicked it next to her hamper. Slipping off her stockings and silk blouse, Claire rummaged around in her closet for something slinky and sophisticated to wear. She chose a deep turquoise dress with a scoop neck. She pulled her hair into a French twist and freshened her makeup. A pair of teardrop silver earrings and her favorite black peekaboo toe shoes completed the look. As she was spritzing on perfume, she heard a knock on her door. A glance at the clock on her nightstand confirmed her suspicion. Darrin and he was exactly on time.

"Hi, sweetheart. I need to grab my purse, and I'll be ready to go," Claire said, kissing him on the cheek.

"I need to talk to you," Darrin said. He walked in and shut the door behind him.

"You sound serious. Let's go into the living room." Claire figured he must be nervous and wanted to ask her in private rather than at the restaurant. Darrin wasn't a fan of public displays of affection. She sat down on the couch. Instead of sitting next to her, Darrin sat opposite her in the chair. "What did you want to talk about?" She gave him an encouraging smile.

"This isn't easy for me. We've been seeing each

other for quite some time, and I think you're amazing." Darrin cleared his throat and swallowed. "And Claire, it's just... I've been seeing somebody else." He looked everywhere but at her.

Shocked, Claire struggled to understand his words, but her head buzzed. "How long?"

"Does that really matter? I mean, what matters is that you and I aren't a good fit. You should just accept that it's over." His face was an unreadable mask. He stood to leave. "I'm sorry."

"No. No, I don't think so. You don't come in here and out of the blue tell me you've been seeing someone else then walk out the door. I'm sorry, but I deserve an explanation. No. Scratch that. I demand an answer. We've been seeing each other for almost a year. I have gone to your boring hospital functions. I've been nice to your mother which is no easy feat, let me tell you. That woman is a hell dragon. I've smiled and schmoozed everyone you told me to schmooze even when they were busy grabbing my butt the minute you turned your back. So, you, Darrin Stanislowski, owe me a freakin' explanation!" Claire's voice rose, and she shook with anger.

"It's not you, Claire. You've been great. You are great. You and I together as a couple are not so great," Darrin said.

His lack of emotion angered Claire. She felt her ears get hot. "It's not me? How could it not be me? You are dumping me on what has already been a horrible day. I deserve an explanation."

"I'm gay. Are you happy?" Darrin yelled back at

her. His words dampened her anger. "I'm tired of hiding who I am. I'm tired of using you to hide it. You deserve better. I knew you were expecting a marriage proposal soon. It's not like you've been subtle. I don't want to live a lie anymore. I'm planning on telling my friends and family, but I felt you deserved to hear it from me first. I'm sorry, Claire. I didn't mean to hurt you." Darrin's unhappiness filled the room.

"You're really gay?" Claire tried to process what he had just told her. "Are you seeing someone, or did you just say that to make it easier for me to hate you?" She tried to wrap her brain around the idea of the man she had been seeing for the past year wasn't who she thought he was.

"I've met someone. He's made me realize that I don't have to live a lie. You would like him, Claire. He's funny and smart. Like you, but a guy. He makes me happy. I want someone to make you happy like that, too." He gave her a sad smile. "I'm sorry that I lied to you. I hope you'll forgive me, and we can be friends."

"Too soon. Listen, can you just go now? I need to be alone. Please, just go." Claire wiped away her angry tears with the back of her hand.

"I understand." Darrin tried to give her a hug, but Claire shrugged him off. He walked out of the apartment and shut the door behind him.

Once Darrin left, Claire sat back down on the sofa and leaned her head back as she tried to accept what she just heard. Her boyfriend of a year had just dumped her for a guy. She got fired from the only job she had ever held. She had less than a month's worth of savings in the bank, and a fifteen-year-old Volvo that was a crap shoot every day on whether it would start. The sum of her life was bleak.

Claire felt a tickle on her cheek. She turned her head to see Ginger sniffing her. She reached up and stroked the kitten's fuzzy head. "Well, Ginger, looks like it's just you and me. What are we going to do?" Ginger leaped down on to Claire's lap and curled up to go to sleep. "You've got the right idea." Claire kicked off her shoes and settled back onto the couch to figure out her next move.

Chapter Two

Claire awoke to kitten whiskers tickling her chin. She gave Gingersnap a quick pat on the head and put her on the ground. A quick glance at the clock told her that she had slept through the night. It was early morning, and the sun was just peeking up over the city's skyline. She went into her small kitchen and started a pot of coffee. She popped a bagel in the toaster and searched through her fridge for cream cheese. Her refrigerator shelves revealed a limp bunch of carrots next to a jar of olives but nothing else. She settled on strawberry jam. Smearing the bagel with a large dollop of jam and pouring a cup of coffee, Claire sat on the bar stool at her kitchen counter. She opened her laptop and searched the online help wanted ads. "Let's see if we can find someplace looking for an out-of-work history major whose only experience is writing advertisements for a pharmaceutical company." Claire tapped away at the keyboard. "Secretary wanted. Must type eighty words per minute. That leaves me out."

Claire spent the next hour browsing through job after job. She realized she wasn't qualified for most positions in the history field. She had dropped out of her master's program halfway through her second year when she landed the position at Gaston Pharmaceuticals thanks to a referral from an ex-boyfriend who used to work there. The money had been good, and she had jumped at the opportunity. Now, she found herself with no job, a useless degree, and no prospects. She closed her laptop and called her mom.

"Hi, Mom. It's me," Claire said with a false cheerfulness.

"You're up bright and early on a Saturday. What's wrong?" Claire's mother, Mary, had a sixth sense when it came to her children.

"Well, let's see. I got fired, found a kitten, and Darrin dumped me for a guy," Claire said. "Other than that, I'm good. And you?"

"Gracious. I didn't expect all of that. Let's back up. Start with getting fired," Mary said.

Claire told her mother all that transpired the day before. When she finished, her mom was silent. "Mom, are you still there?"

"Sorry, dear. I was thinking. An odd thing happened the other day, and I haven't talked to you about it. Aunt Rose left the farm to me and it's vacant. It's not much, but she left her farm and a small yearly allowance to operate it with the stipulation it stay in the family. I would venture to say that you have no savings, and now that Darrin is out of the picture, nothing to keep you in the city."

"Harsh. I wouldn't say nothing. I have friends and a life and..." Claire trailed off as it dawned on her. "Mom, are you suggesting I move to Aunt Rose's farm? In the country? With cows and chickens and who knows what else?"

"Why not? The house and farm need sorted out and you could go for the short term while you figure out what you want to do. Expensive shoes and a nice wardrobe won't pay your electric bill. Plus, you'd be helping me out. I don't have time to go up there to go through the house until the end of the school year. This is a win-win for you and me." Mary was an elementary school teacher and used to having her directions followed. "Your father can't do it with his busy practice. Your sister is up to her eyeballs in wedding plans and your brother won't be back from Africa for at least three months. It makes sense."

"Let me think about it. Everything just happened yesterday. I haven't even had time to sort it out in my brain or see if I can even get another job. The only time I've been to the country is when we visited Aunt Rose when I was a kid. A bee stung me, and I swelled up like a puffer fish. It wasn't a good experience. Cows and chickens don't like me." Claire envisioned living in the country in her Ferragamo boots. It just wouldn't work.

"Don't think about it too long. Someone needs to head up and get the keys from the attorneys and make sure the house is still standing. A neighbor has been taking care of the animals and checking on the house, but I am sure he doesn't want to continue. Consider it a retreat. A chance to rethink the direction of your life. Regroup." Claire's father was a psychologist, and his psychobabble worked its way into her mom's vocabulary.

"Give me a few days. I'll talk to you later, Mom. Love you," Claire said as she disconnected the call before her mother could say anything else. She was a city girl through and through. She loved the sounds and smells of the city streets. The bright lights and crowds were part of her. She couldn't imagine not being able to get to a Starbucks in less than a few blocks.

Claire needed a second opinion. She called Isabella.

"Isabella's House of Chaos. How can I be driven insane today?" Isabella answered. "Claire, I swear if these kids don't settle down, I will lose my mind. We need a spa day."

"Good morning to you, too. So, I will not be Mrs. Stanislowski. In fact, no one will be Mrs. Stanislowski. It will end up being Dr. Darrin Stanislowski and Mr. Stanislowski." Claire grimaced as the image of Darrin slipping a diamond ring on another man's hairy knuckles formed in her mind. She wanted him to be happy, but it hurt that he'd lied to her for so long.

"What the heck are you talking about?" Isabella demanded.

"Darrin needed to talk last night alright. He came out last night. I'm the first person he told. He dumped me. I'm okay with him being who he needs to be, but I'm gob smacked. I lost my job and my boyfriend in one day. This is what I get for cursing the universe. Now my mom wants me to go live on my Great Aunt Rose's farm and sort out her estate."

"Crap on a cracker. I knew something was off about your relationship, but even I didn't see that one coming. I would love to have been a fly on the wall to see that meltdown. How badly did you hurt him?" Isabella asked.

"I didn't even raise my voice. Okay, I yelled a little, but can you blame me? I did not see this coming at all. I was a gay man's beard and a clueless idiot. I really liked Darrin. I could have loved him."

"But you didn't love him. I thought he was uptight. I would never have guessed Darrin was gay. And your mom is crazy if she thinks you would survive in the country. She didn't see you freak out when a pigeon came too close to you at the park. I thought you would hyperventilate and pass out from fear. A chicken would give you a stroke." Isabella chuckled.

"I don't like pigeons. They are dirty birds. And I could survive in the country if I had to, but I prefer the city. I haven't even had a day to look for a job. I'll find something. Worse comes to worst, I'll swing up to Cosner's Creek to make sure the farm is still standing then head back home," Claire said. She poured herself another cup of coffee and stirred the last bit of sugar she scraped from the sugar bowl. She needed to get groceries and some kitten food for Gingersnap.

"Don't do anything rash. You've had a crummy twenty-four hours. I know you, chica, and you will do something crazy you'll regret later. As your friend, I am telling you, don't do it."

"I won't do anything crazy. I've got to go. My kitten needs food," Claire said.

"Come by later today and I'll feed you. I'll make chile rellenos and flan just for you. Comfort food is a must in these trying times. Talk to you later." Isabella knew the way to Claire's heart was food.

Claire didn't cook. She microwaved, tossed salads, and made spaghetti but that was the extent of her kitchen skills. She gave Ginger a small amount of tuna from a can, then went to take a shower. Once she toweled off, she pulled on an old sweatshirt. She yanked a pair of yoga pants and socks out of her gym bag, sniffed them, and decided they could last at least another day. Mentally, she added laundry to her to-do list for the day. Grabbing her keys, she walked down to the street and hopped into her Volvo. She turned the key and the engine roared to life. She put it into drive and as she pulled out, the Volvo gave a horrible clunk, the check engine light came on, and it shuddered to a stop. Claire tried to start it again. Nothing happened. She climbed out of the car and called the garage that did her oil changes and tune-ups.

Twenty minutes later, a tow truck pulled up and Iggy hopped out. His dad owned the garage, but Iggy had taken over the day-to-day operations a year ago after his dad's heart attack. "What's up, Miss O'Connor? Car won't start?" Iggy chomped away at a piece of gum. His greasy black hair spiked into hard points gave him the look of a crazed hedgehog. His face was pockmarked, and he had a large beaked nose. Tattoos decorated every inch of his arms. If Claire hadn't known him for years, she would have crossed the street to avoid him. Iggy was a decent guy.

"I pulled out and it gave a loud kerplunk. Then it died and wouldn't start back up," Claire shrugged her shoulders. "I don't know what's wrong with her." She handed Iggy her keys. He slid into the driver's seat and tried to start the car. Nothing happened. He hopped out and opened the hood. He fiddled with some wires and gave an occasional grunt. "How bad is it?"

"It ain't good. I'll tow her to the shop. It looks like the timing belt and that is bad. It could be the death of this old girl." Iggy patted the hood of the car like it was an old horse.

"I can't afford a new car," Claire wailed. "Heck, I can't afford this car if it's an expensive repair."

"I can't make you any promises. I'll call you later today and tell you the damage," Iggy said. "I won't charge you for the tow. It's just down the block anyway."

"Thanks, Iggy. Do your best." Claire's shoulders slumped as she realized that her bad luck wasn't over. She headed down the street to walk to the market. It was only five blocks, and the walk would clear her head. Someone was trying to tell her something. She had no job, no man, no money, and now, no car. Her grandma said bad luck came in threes, so she was due some good luck. Maybe she should buy a lottery ticket. She kicked at a soda can in the middle of the sidewalk.

"Ma'am, there's no littering," A voice said from behind her. Startled, Claire turned and saw a police officer. He pulled out a book and a pen from his back pocket. "I'll have to write you a ticket."

"But...I... oh, never mind." Claire gave a dejected sigh and gave him her name and address. She snatched the ticket from his hand the second he reached out to hand it to her.

Claire walked the remaining few blocks to the market, picked up a bag of kitten food, and a few other essentials and headed home. When she opened her apartment door, Gingersnap ran up to greet her. "You know what, Ginger? I think the universe has been beating me over the head the past two days and telling me it is time to make a change. How about you and I take a little trip to the country?"

Continue the story and discover the mystery on Kindle Vella - Amazon's home to serialized stories.

Please consider leaving a review. Small, independent authors and artists appreciate your support! Thank you.

About the Author

After a career in libraries, Amy E. Lilly decided it was time to actually read and write books rather than push them on her unsuspecting patrons. She lives in Virginia with her husband, two cats, two dogs, five goats, and six chickens.

www.ingramcontent.com/pod-product-compliance
Lightning Source LLC
Chambersburg PA
CBHW070606120726
47909CB00007B/2464